RETURN

Mary Rice

SOLASTA BOOKS

Return

By

Mary Rice

Cover art courtesy of FrinaArt

Solasta Books
Charlotte, North Carolina

Visit the website for more novels by M H Rice, including more books in the Switch series.
MHRicebooks.com

ISBN 978-0-9995917-2-7

SWITCH TRILOGY

SWITCH

FORSAKEN

RETURN

Other Books by Mary Rice

THE SECRET OF PROPHET HOUSE

TAPESTRY (COMING SOON!)

To Bill, who has always been my Ethan.

And to my sister, Patty, who died too young.

Nova closed her eyes and tried to shut out the sounds around her. And there it was. The almost imperceptible tug. *Oh my God. I can still feel it...*

CHAPTER 1

Nova lay in bed, listening to the sounds of the garden while her mind replayed her conversation with Ethan. He'd been understanding as always. He hadn't pushed her for more information than she was willing to give, even though he'd obviously noticed she was holding back. She was tempted to call him again, just to hear his voice, but resisted the urge. Maybe it was better not to lean on him so much. What was the point? Soon her life would change and they'd be starting over again. Besides, she needed time to adjust to being back at Willow Hill, back to the night she'd traveled. Smoothing things out with Ethan could wait.

Part of her still felt as if she could close her eyes and wake up at home in Connecticut with Ethan beside her on the bed and Alana sleeping peacefully in the next room, unaware that her life would soon be wiped out as if it had never happened. It was a cruel thing but only temporary. At least, Nova prayed it was.

She put her hands over her face as the weight of what she'd done crashed in on her. There had been no other way to right things, but that knowledge did nothing to soothe the pain in her heart or the twisting sensation in her gut. She felt her pulse speeding up and took several deep breaths, trying to stave off the panic attack that threatened to take hold of her. Her heartbeat pounded in her ears as the cruel voice in her head screamed, *Stupid! You've made another mistake, and now you'll never see your sister again!*

What if it were true? Alana would never have the life she deserved, her brilliant light snuffed out for all eternity. Already the image of her sister had dimmed a little. Why was it happening so fast? Nova squeezed her eyes shut and tried to picture Alana—hazel eyes, golden hair, her mouth curving up slightly at the edges. Nova could vividly imagine each feature individually, but the whole picture took minutes to form. She knew from experience that it would only get worse. Eventually, Alana would fade into the shadows of her brain—just an imaginary friend from childhood. Not a real person who'd had dreams of her own and wasn't afraid of anything.

Nova shook herself mentally. Aunt Jean had said that you always remembered the people you knew in other lives. And besides, she'd never really forgotten Alana. It was just that until now, she'd never known her sister past age five. That had to be why, in another life, she'd thought of her as an imaginary friend and not a real person. Her young brain hadn't been mature enough to retain all of the memories of her sister.

Still, there was no denying that Alana's image was fading, like a slowly developing Polaroid picture, only backward. Nova concentrated, summoning her sister's face again. This time it popped up in her brain right away. She smiled, satisfied for now.

"I promise I won't forget you, Allie," she whispered.

But if Nova was going to get her back, it would have to be soon. The more time that passed, the harder it would be. She took a deep breath and held it, forcing her heart rate to slow to a more normal pace. She let the air out of her lungs and willed away the negative voice. *Anything is possible...* she repeated over and over in her head.

The thought of visiting the tapestry again crossed her mind. It was tempting. Surely at least one reality included both of her siblings. She could stay in until she found it. If all else failed, she could jump back and forth between lives. One life with her sister and one with Marshall. She wondered how long it would take for her to go completely mad if she jumped from timeline to timeline over and over. *Dangerous.* Maybe her great-grandmother had known from experience.

It was unsettling to think that she could be dabbling in a power that her great-grandmother had warned them about. Out of everyone in the family, Evelyn Grant had apparently known more about traveling than anyone. She must have had a reason for keeping the tapestry to herself.

But it made no sense. There were endless possibilities there. It had allowed Nova to go back to where she'd started long after she should have been able to. She'd plucked her little brother from the jaws of oblivion. He was restored. Good as new. How could that be bad?

She felt a shudder go up her spine as, once again, her great-grandmother's word played in her head, this time accompanied by a dark sense of foreboding. *Dangerous.* Nova did her best to shake it off, but her mind fought her by replaying the warning over and over.

Stop! She sat up and took several deep breaths. That was when she felt it—a gentle but persistent pull. The tapestry had not fully released its hold on her. She felt it tugging, as if they were connected by an invisible cord. It was a strange sensation. If she relaxed and let herself drift, would she find herself back there? That was an alarming thought. Visiting on purpose was one thing, but being dragged back against her will was quite another. And yet there it was, subtly trying to draw her in again.

She closed her eyes and mentally forced it back, hoping the pull would fade in time. After all, traveling was traveling. The same rules should apply no matter how you did it. At least, she hoped so. The thought of being tethered to the tapestry forever was unsettling to say the least. If she let her guard down, would it really drag her back? *Dangerous…*

—

8

She shivered. "Okay, Evelyn. I hear you."

The house had been quiet for at least an hour, except for the sounds drifting in through the open window—mostly crickets with an occasional hoot from an owl in search of its nightly meal. She swung her legs over the side of the bed and dropped lightly to the floor. Her jeans and pale-pink top were on the chair where she'd discarded them when she'd been in this timeline before. It seemed like ages ago.

She pulled them on, opened her door, and peered into the hallway. The landing at the staircase glowed slightly from a nightlight at the top, obviously intended to prevent some poor sleepwalker from tumbling down in the dead of night. The rest of the expansive hallway was nearly black as ink. It didn't matter. Nova knew exactly where she was going.

Certain her little brother would be asleep by now, she slipped out of her room and padded quietly down the hall, pausing at the top of the stairs to listen. Still no sound except for the clock. The steady tick tock drifted up the hall from the direction of her room. There were several other rooms in that part of the house beyond hers. One was Aunt Jean's bedroom, but she had no idea what the other closed doors led to. They would bear exploring… but not tonight.

She proceeded, running her hand along the wall, until she came to a door that was slightly ajar. Marshall insisted that his bedroom door be kept open at Aunt Jean's. He slept with it closed at home, but that was a familiar environment. Willow Hill was huge compared to their house, with closed-off rooms they'd never explored. She had to admit that the thought of someone hiding in one of those rooms gave her the creeps as well. Nova guessed that her little brother wanted to make sure their parents would hear him if he called out during the night.

She gave it a push, and the door swung open the rest of the way. A soft light from the full moon spilled in through the window and illuminated the room just enough for Nova to make out his form in the bed. She heard him breathing slowly in and out, deeply asleep. "The sleep of the dead" was what her dad always called it, claiming that a freight train could pass by, just feet away, without waking Marshall.

Nova tiptoed to the side of the bed. In the moonlight, he seemed even younger than his nine years. He was sprawled on top of the covers as if he'd leapt for the bed and lost consciousness on the way down. That was typical for him. Marshall's engine was in overdrive all day long, but when it shut down, that was it. There was no rousing him. What goes up must eventually come down, and he was definitely down—passed out cold.

"I'm glad you're back, kiddo," she whispered, brushing his hair back slightly from his face. Her fingers came away with a piece of hay, and she had to stifle a laugh.

A floorboard in the hall creaked. She held her breath and froze. Then softly, from just outside the doorway, came, "What are you doing in here, Nova?"

Nova let the air out of her lungs. "Nothing, Aunt Jean." She backed away from Marshall and closed his bedroom door as she stepped into the hall. "I just felt like checking on him. I wasn't tired…"

She shifted her weight and waited for Aunt Jean to say something else, but her aunt stood in the dark hallway without saying a word. Nova couldn't see her face, but she had the distinct feeling that her aunt knew she was lying.

When the silence became awkward, Nova spoke up. "I guess I'll go back to bed." She turned to head back to her room.

"Wait," Aunt Jean said quickly. She flicked on a tiny flashlight. "I keep this on my bedside table." She pointed the beam down the hall toward the staircase. "How does hot chocolate sound? It always helps me sleep."

Nova wasn't fooled. Her aunt wanted to talk. She thought about mentioning that chocolate was loaded with caffeine and would most likely not help anyone sleep but thought better of it.

"Sure, I guess." She wasn't ready to share her experience in the other timeline just yet but didn't see a way out of it and dutifully followed her aunt down the stairs and into the kitchen.

Aunt Jean flicked on the overhead lights, and the kitchen lit up. After being in the dark, Nova had to blink several times before her eyes adjusted. Everything looked exactly the same as she remembered. She hadn't really expected anything to change, but there was always that possibility. It was comforting to see that it hadn't. Half of a chocolate layer cake sat in the glass cake holder on the counter. Her aunt had made it the day she traveled, and they'd all had a piece that night at dinner. A few hours later, Nova had gone upstairs and ended up back in Connecticut in another timeline. Nova shuddered. What was her aunt going to say about what she'd done?

Aunt Jean busied herself heating milk on the stove. She melted chocolate in another pot over low heat, then whisked it into the hot milk, adding a splash of vanilla extract at the end. It smelled heavenly. Nova had never had hot chocolate that didn't come from a packet poured into boiling water. But then, Aunt Jean made everything from scratch.

When the cups were filled and marshmallows were added, she motioned for Nova to sit on the bench at the massive table before taking a seat in the armchair on the end. She leaned forward and looked Nova in the eye.

"Now, tell me what's going on," she said firmly.

CHAPTER 2

Nova pretended to be engrossed in her hot chocolate, watching the marshmallows slowly turn to mounds of white fluff. She felt her aunt staring at her as she took a sip and came away with a marshmallow mustache.

Aunt Jean chuckled and handed her a napkin. "Well?"

"Nothing's going on. I wasn't sleepy. That's all."

"Hmm. Let's try this another way. What would you think if you found your nearly sixteen-year-old great-niece sitting by her nine-year-old brother in the middle of the night, watching him sleep?"

"I'd wonder if I'd traveled ahead about fifty or sixty years."

Aunt Jean threw her head back and laughed. "Honey, you sure know how to tickle my funny bone. But you're not getting off the hook that easily. Have you done something I don't know about?"

Nova cleared her throat nervously. "You know I traveled and brought Alana back, right?"

Aunt Jean's face lost any trace of humor. "When was this?"

"Tonight. Well, not exactly. It's hard to explain." Nova's stomach knotted up. Maybe her aunt didn't know because she'd been dead in that life.

Aunt Jean closed her eyes and sat perfectly still. The muscles in her jaw twitched slightly as she concentrated.

When she didn't speak for a couple of minutes, Nova touched her aunt's shoulder and her eyes flew open.

Aunt Jean looked confused. "You'll have to tell me about it."

Nova sighed, wishing she'd stayed in her room. The thought of reliving the whole experience in the other timeline made her want to crawl into a hole. She'd already done this with Ethan, and it had been exhausting, though she hadn't told him everything. Her aunt would never settle for the watered-down version Nova had given him. She'd want to know everything.

Aunt Jean was drumming her fingers impatiently on the table. Whether Nova was up to sharing or not, there was clearly no way around it.

Nova cleared her throat. "We were all on the porch that night—I mean *tonight*—and I left to go upstairs."

"Yes, I know. You said you were going to bed."

"Well... I'd been thinking about traveling all day. Planning what I would do."

"You were planning to travel? Without telling me?" Aunt Jean frowned.

Nova took a gulp of hot chocolate and felt it searing her esophagus all the way down. It took her a second to recover. "I'm sorry." She swallowed again—hard. "I should have talked to you about it. I know that now."

Nova stared at her cup without taking another drink. After another awkward silence, she looked up. Her aunt was studying her, an odd look on her face. She was still frowning but didn't exactly look angry.

"Go on, honey."

Nova started to take another drink but stopped herself just in time. She could still feel the burn from the first swig.

"Nova..."

"Sorry. Okay, at first I lay in bed listening to the clock. I could feel something happening, like I was floating. Then I had a clear vision of Alana. It was like she was really there, motioning for me to come on. I'd only seen pictures of her when she was little, but in my vision, she was my age."

"You saw pictures of your sister?"

"Not pictures actually. Drawings. Dad had lots of them in his office. I found them when I was snooping around in there."

"When was that?"

"After Dad traveled ahead in time and I woke up here too. I didn't know why he was back, so I looked around his office when my parents were at school with Marshall. I was hoping I'd find something that would explain why he was alive and why so many things were different."

"And you found drawings of your sister."

"Yes. And her birth and death certificates. Except he'd drawn pictures of her when she was five, but her death certificate said she'd died a couple of hours after she was born. I was so confused. I didn't know about timelines or traveling, so none of it made sense. And that still didn't explain why Dad was alive."

"No, I guess not. But we can talk about that later." Aunt Jean seemed impatient again. "Let's get back on track. You saw a vision of your sister, only she was older, like you."

"Right. I kind of stayed there for a minute, watching her. I wanted to follow her, but I guess I held back, because nothing happened at first. Not until you came in and told me to let go."

Aunt Jean's eyes widened. "I did what?"

"You came into my room. I heard you walk in. I wasn't sure it was you until you touched my face and told me to let go. And I did. I traveled. Don't you remember?"

Her aunt's frown deepened. "Let's get past that for now too. Tell me what happened next." She was clearly not willing talk about her role in the matter.

"Okay." Nova cleared her throat again. "I imagined my sixteenth birthday with my twin sister. Both of us were there. I could picture it clearly. And that's what I aimed for. When I woke up, I was back home and Alana was alive."

"That's it? You just thought of her being there on your birthday?"

"Yeah, I guess so." Nova tried to collect her thoughts. "At first, I wasn't sure of what I'd done. I knew I'd traveled, but I had no idea what to expect. I went to the office to make sure Dad was there, but the office was Alana's room." Nova smiled, remembering the moment she'd seen her sister for the first time. "She came in and put her hands over my eyes. She thought I was crying because of some guy named Steven. I couldn't believe she was there. It was amazing." Nova felt tears run down her cheeks. She hadn't realized she was crying now too. She wiped them away with the back of her hand.

Aunt Jean sat back in the armchair and shook her head. "You saved your sister after all these years? You don't know how many times I've wanted to do something about her. But you took matters into your own hands." She looked at Nova with utter admiration. "I can't believe it." Her expression changed to one of confusion and she leaned forward again. "But she's not here now. What happened?"

Without thinking, Nova swallowed another gulp of hot chocolate and felt the heat all the way down again. "I didn't stay there. I came back to this timeline."

"Why?"

Nova looked at her hands clasped around the mug of hot chocolate and thought about her dad's coffee cup shattered on the floor. "I had to. I mean I had to undo what I'd done. Marshall wasn't in that timeline."

"Ah… well, that certainly is a problem." Aunt Jean stared at her own cup for a few seconds. "Let me get this straight. You traveled to a different timeline—one where your sister hadn't died. But when you got there, you found out that your little brother had vanished from reality. Is that right?"

Nova nodded. "That's right. He was never born."

Aunt Jean sounded tired when she said, "I guess that makes sense. Your parents had two children to take care of instead of one. It's logical to assume that would impact their desire to have another child." She squeezed Nova's hand. "I'm sorry, honey. I know how you must be feeling. It's not fair, is it?"

Nova felt another tear run down her cheek and brushed it away. "No."

Aunt Jean seemed deep in thought, so Nova sat quietly, relieved she didn't have to talk.

Finally her aunt spoke up. "So you just visited that life." It wasn't really a question.

Nova shifted her weight on the bench. "I didn't visit. Not exactly."

"What do you mean?"

"After I traveled, I didn't know about Marshall right away. Neither did Dad. Sometimes Marshall doesn't want to get up in the morning. We have to drag him out of bed. I know that's probably hard to believe since he's up at the crack of dawn here, but that's because of the horses. At home, he's not always a morning person. The door to his room next to mine was closed. Dad found out before I did because he went to get him up and he was gone. His room wasn't his room anymore. It was the office. I was out with Ethan, so I found out when I got back. After that, it took a while to figure out what to do." Nova resisted the urge to add, "Because you were dead and couldn't help us."

Aunt Jean sat up straight. "How long were you there?"

"About a week, I guess."

"A week?" She sounded incredulous. "Child, how did you get back?"

Nova stared at the mug of chocolate in front of her. The marshmallows had nearly disappeared, leaving behind a rim of foam around the inside of the cup. She thought about taking another drink to buy some time but wasn't sure she'd be able to get it down. Her great-grandmother's warning rang in her mind again. There would be no going back once she said it. But if she couldn't tell Aunt Jean, who *could* she tell?

Nova took a deep breath. "I used the tapestry."

CHAPTER 3

Her aunt was thunderstruck. She stared at Nova, her mouth hanging open. Nova was tempted to make the catching flies joke but thought better of it. Clearly, the tapestry was something you didn't joke about.

"The tapestry…" Aunt Jean said almost too softly to hear. She was holding on to the table as if she expected to room to pitch around them.

Nova laid her hand on her aunt's arm. "Have you ever been there?"

She shook her head solemnly. "Mother talked about it a few times but always in vague terms. When Kate and I became interested and asked questions, she told us it wasn't something we needed to know about, that we had plenty to do just keeping up with one timeline. After that, she never mentioned it again, even though I tried to get her to. I wanted to know. After a while, I started thinking that maybe it wasn't real."

Nova was shocked. Evelyn had obviously known about the tapestry. She must have visited it herself, because she'd written about it in her journal. Why wouldn't she have told her daughters how to use it? Or how to get there? The word her great-grandmother had written in her journal popped into Nova's head again. *Dangerous.* She shook it off and looked her aunt in the eye. "It's real."

"Tell me what it was like." Aunt Jean's voice had

taken on a childlike quality, like a six-year-old version of herself was asking Nova to tell her about the North Pole.

Nova thought for a moment. How could she describe something so incredible? It was like trying to describe the sun. Aunt Jean sat on the edge of her seat, waiting expectantly, and Nova realized that must have been how she had looked when Aunt Jean first talked about time travel in the garden—awestruck. Temporarily tongue-tied, Nova tried to figure out a way to adequately put the tapestry into words.

Aunt Jean's patience had apparently worn thin. "If you don't tell me something soon, I'm going to burst. And believe me, you don't want to see that."

"I'm sorry. It's hard to describe." She took a deep breath. "Okay, from a distance, it looked kind of like a massive silver cloud that was lit up from the inside."

"From a distance?"

"Yes. I went into the tunnel, like you do when you travel. But instead of aiming at a memory or a destination, I waited there. My mind threw all these images at me, almost like it was trying to force me to make a choice. I know that sounds weird, but that's exactly what it was like. I finally managed to stop it."

"How?"

"I don't know exactly. The best way to describe it is that I pushed the visions away with my mind. Does that even make sense?"

Her aunt nodded.

"Once the images were gone, I found myself in total blackness. There was nothing there. Not even the tiniest bit of light. I couldn't feel anything around me either. I was just floating in this void. It was terrifying at first. I thought I might be stuck there forever. "

"I don't blame you for being frightened," Aunt Jean said softly.

"My head hurt too."

"That could have been from the concussion."

"Oh!" Nova felt the side of her head, and there they were—stitches. "I forgot…"

"You forgot about hitting your head?"

"No. I just—"

"It didn't happen in the other timeline," Aunt Jean jumped in impatiently, obviously anxious for her to continue.

"Right. Anyway, after a while, my headache went away, and I wasn't really that scared anymore. I don't know why, except that I felt like something was coming. Like all I had to do was pull back a curtain and I'd see it. I kept moving forward and, all of a sudden, I saw it and I felt… I don't know… wonder." Even now, a chill ran up her spine from thinking about that moment.

"Wonder," her aunt repeated wistfully. "That's a good word. And all this time you were moving toward it?"

"Yes!"

"How?"

Nova thought for a moment. Moving toward the tapestry had been effortless. She couldn't remember anything she'd done to propel herself through the darkness.

"I don't know for sure. It just happened. Mom and Dad took Marshall and me to the water park in New Haven a few years ago. My favorite part was the lazy river. You could sit in a giant inner tube and float along with the current. It was like that. "

"I remember my mother saying once that the tapestry will pull you in if you let it. She said it more to herself than to me. That was the last time she ever mentioned it."

That made sense. If she hadn't floated toward it by her own power, then it must have been the tapestry. Nova felt the hairs stand up on the back of her neck.

"Tell me the rest," Aunt Jean prodded.

Nova shook off the uneasy feeling. "When I got closer, it looked more like a giant spider web than a tapestry, with thousands of glowing silver threads. But when I was inside it, I saw that the strands weren't all the same color exactly. They had slightly different tints, depending on whose timeline I was looking at."

"So the threads weren't just yours? Some belonged to different travelers?"

"Yeah. At least, that's what I think. Because mine were all the same color. I hadn't really thought about whether or not the strands belonged to other travelers. Maybe everyone in your life has a strand, or timeline, but travelers are the only ones who know about it."

"That makes sense." Aunt Jean nodded. "It's comforting, isn't it? Knowing that all our loved ones are there with us."

"Mine are blue."

Aunt Jean gave her a questioning look. "Your *what* are blue?"

"My timelines. They're blue. I recognized them right away. I don't know how, but I did."

Aunt Jean smiled. "You've always liked blue, I bet."

Nova was taken aback. Blue *had* always been her favorite color. "Ha! You're right. What's your favorite color, Aunt Jean?"

Her aunt's smile widened. "Have you noticed the flowers in my garden? I'd bet my strands are tinted yellow." She chuckled.

While the garden was sprinkled with pinks, lavenders, purples, and reds, the most prominent flowers were yellow. Aunt Jean was obviously partial to them—yellow roses, marigolds, daylilies, black-eyed Susans, begonias, daisies, and even a few sunflowers. Determined to make a gardener out of her great-niece, Aunt Jean had taken special care to point them all out by name several times. Even so, Nova was surprised her brain had retained the information.

Aunt Jean cocked her head. "You look amused. What's funny?"

"I must have the weirdest brain. I can remember all the flowers you showed me in the garden. It's like cerebrospinal fluid."

"What on earth are you talking about?"

"After I hit my head on the driveway at home, I lay there with Dad holding my head, and I felt something dripping down my face and onto the concrete. We had just taken a test in biology, and one of the questions was to name three ingredients in cerebrospinal fluid. I couldn't remember even one at the time. But when I was lying there with my head bleeding, I remembered. I still can. Glucose, sodium chloride, and protein."

Aunt Jean chuckled. "It doesn't sound that strange to me. We have heightened awareness when we're stressed. You were stressed then, and you are now. That's why it's important to talk about what happened right away instead of waiting until you have time to calm down. Your memory might not be as sharp later."

"I guess so. I can remember hitting my head, but I don't remember the hospital very well. That feels more like a dream."

"Unfortunately, that's the way it works when you travel. The more time that passes, the more your memory fades."

"But I'm back in the same timeline and it all just happened. Shouldn't I remember everything?"

"Of course you'll remember a lot because you *are* in the same timeline. But the one you traveled to and then left… that one will fade over time."

"That's depressing. I want to remember it all."

Aunt Jean patted her hand. "That's just the way it is, honey. Nothing can be done about it. Let's focus on where we are now and what we plan to do."

"Okay." Nova's mind replayed the contents of spinal fluid. Maybe she'd get an opportunity to take that test again and this time she'd get it right. *I'm so weird…* Nova felt the urge to laugh but suppressed it.

"Tell me more about the tapestry," her aunt urged.

Nova's heart raced just thinking about being there again. "It's the most beautiful thing you've ever seen. The strands glow... all these different shades. When you find yours, you can see how so many others have intersected with each one and influenced the direction of that timeline."

"So I guess the tapestry you saw was yours."

Nova sat up straight. "What do you mean?"

"Well, honey, unless God made you the center of the universe, the tapestry you were in was made up of your timelines intersecting others—"

"You're right! I hadn't thought of that! Of course there must be millions of other tapestries!"

Aunt Jean patted her hand again. "Let's not wake the whole house." She chuckled.

Nova fought off her excitement and lowered her voice. "It's amazing to think that it's not one tapestry with all of us in it. We all have our own and they cross over into others! I saw so many timelines from other people whose tapestries intersected with mine. That's why it seemed to go on forever. Maybe if I'd kept going deeper into it—"

"Let's stop there," her aunt cautioned. "I'm beginning to think we're treading on dangerous ground. I don't think we're supposed to meddle in other people's timelines. That's probably why my mother didn't talk to us about it."

"In her journal, Evelyn said some powers are dangerous. I guess that's what she was talking about. Still..." Nova shook her head. "It's awesome to think about, isn't it? All the different tapestries..."

"It is, honey. There are billions of galaxies in the universe. We just happen to be in one of them." Aunt Jean leaned forward again, her arms resting on the table. "You still haven't told me how you used yours to get back here."

Nova smiled. "If you touch one of your strands, you can see inside that life at that exact moment. I can't describe how incredible it is. I saw myself walking through a museum with my dad somewhere in Europe!" She waited for that image to sink in. "I visited so many of my possible lives. It was like watching myself in a movie, but not a normal movie where it always goes the same way. It was like watching a movie that you could change over and over. Part of me wanted to stay there."

"Did you?" Aunt Jean frowned. "Interesting."

"Yes! It's hard to explain. You almost *forget* why you're there." Nova frowned. "That's not exactly right. It's more like you're being pulled in so many directions with so many possibilities that you can't concentrate on anything else. You have to know what's in the next one and the next one. It's hard to stop looking."

Aunt Jean nodded. "It sounds overwhelming."

"It is. But it's exciting too. Haven't you ever wondered what other lives you could have had?"

"I guess everyone wonders that now and then. But I've made a lot of changes over the years, and I like where I am now."

"I know, Aunt Jean. It's just incredible to see yourself living in so many different realities. But in the end, I wanted to come back. Even if it meant not having Alana for now. Because I couldn't live with knowing I'd killed my brother."

"No, you couldn't leave things as they were. You were right to come back."

"I still want a life with my sister too though. I can't bear to think about losing her forever. I planned to go back to where I started and try again. Do you think I'll be able to do that? Have my whole family?"

Aunt Jean took Nova's hand and looked her in the eyes. "I think anything is possible, but let's not rush this time, okay?"

"Okay."

"Tell me what happened when you found yourself in the new timeline. Were you still here? At Willow Hill?"

"No. I was back home in bed." Some of that timeline had already faded. It was hard to remember small details, but she could vividly picture waking in her bed at home. "I could tell things were different of course. My room wasn't exactly the same, and my hair was longer. The stitches in my head were gone." She felt them under her hair again. With the swelling and soreness gone, she'd forgotten they were even there.

"And you saw your sister," Aunt Jean said wistfully. "How wonderful that must have been."

"It was." Nova nodded. "I didn't see her at first though. I went into her room, and she came up behind me. She had no idea what had happened…"

"And you never told her?"

"Not at first. I did later though." Nova smiled. "She's a traveler too. We even practiced."

Aunt Jean laughed out loud, immediately clamping her hand over her mouth. "No, you didn't!" she whispered.

"We did! It's your fault, you know." Nova laughed. "If you hadn't let me practice, I might not have had the nerve to do it."

"How far did you travel?"

"Just a little way back." Nova blushed when she thought of kissing Ethan at her window as her sister burst into the room.

"Amazing!" Aunt Jean chuckled. "You girls would be a handful together."

"Alana would at least. She's a lot more impulsive than I am."

"She's like Marshall."

"Yeah."

Aunt Jean shoved her chair back. "Okay, that's enough for tonight. Let's get some sleep. Mornings come early around here, or haven't you noticed?"

"Yeah. I've noticed." Nova stood, suddenly feeling as though all she wanted to do was to crawl into the four-poster and let her brain rest. When she reached the doorway, she looked back. "Aren't you coming?"

"I'll be up in a bit. You run along now."

Nova hesitated. "Aunt Jean?"

"Hmm?"

"Why didn't you know I'd traveled? Don't other travelers always know?"

"That's a good question. I'll have to think about that one."

"Okay. I love you, Aunt Jean."

"I love you too, honey."

Nova turned and headed upstairs. She fell asleep the moment her head hit the pillow. The last thing she heard was the clock.

CHAPTER 4

The next morning, Marshall came barreling into her room and jumped on her bed.

"Wake up, Nova!" He was already dressed in jeans, a tee shirt, and boots.

"Marshall! You scared me half to death. And get those boots off my bed." She grabbed her little brother and tickled him until he broke away, laughing.

"Sorry about my boots. I knocked most of the dirt off though. See?" He held up his foot so she could inspect it. They were mostly clean, but a clump of what appeared to be straw mixed with manure was wedged into the sole.

"Maybe you shouldn't wear them in the house, kiddo." She smiled.

Marshall eyed her suspiciously. "You aren't usually this nice when I wake you up."

"Well, you're a pretty cool brother. Maybe I finally figured that out."

Marshall seemed immensely pleased. "Justin and me are gonna go trail riding this morning. He says I'm ready. You wanna come?"

"Riding, huh? I don't think so. I haven't been taking lessons like you have, you know." The thought of riding a horse was scary enough in a ring. Being on a horse in the woods, with no fence, made a shiver run up her spine.

"Don't be scared." Marshall put his arm around her.

"I'll take care of you."

Nova almost burst into tears. How could she say no, especially after she'd nearly annihilated him? "Okay. But you have to promise you'll protect me."

"Deal." He beamed, obviously delighted by her change of heart.

"And let's eat first. If I'm about to die, I at least want to do it on a full stomach."

Marshall was out the door and down the stairs before Nova's feet hit the floor. She dressed in jeans and a light-blue top, then pulled her hair into a ponytail. *Might as well look nice for the paramedics.* When she finally made it to the kitchen, a stack of steaming hot pancakes covered in syrup was at her place at the table.

"Marshall said you don't want to risk your life on an empty stomach." Aunt Jean laughed.

Nova glanced around the room, but her little brother was nowhere to be seen. "Don't tell me he's already gone to the barn!"

"I've never seen a child eat so fast." Her aunt chuckled. "You'd better hurry up, or he'll be bringing your horse to the house."

Nova groaned. "I can't believe I got myself into this. If I die, give Marshall the *Time Machine* poster on my wall at home. He thinks one-eyed George is funny."

"You probably won't die, but I'll make sure he gets it if you do."

Nova huffed. "I don't know how to ride, and I have no interest in learning."

"It's not that hard. Besides, you're just going to walk the trails. I think you'll enjoy it once you get there."

"If you say so." Nova wasn't convinced.

She took her time eating her pancakes, cutting tiny bites and chewing each one deliberately until nothing but syrup was left on her plate. She thought of asking for seconds, but her stomach already felt as if she'd swallowed a bowling ball. Maybe her mom would think of something else she had to do. It was at least worth a try.

"Where's Mom?" she asked hopefully.

"She went into town with Connie right before you came down. I swear, every day those two think of something else the baby just *has* to have. Your mom's going to make a doting grandmother someday."

"Great," Nova said dejectedly.

Dayton came in the back door wearing dirty boots, jeans, and a gray tee shirt with a tear in one sleeve. Her father looked like a grown-up version of Marshall. "Any pancakes left?"

"Dayton Grant, all you do is eat!" Aunt Jean laughed.

"Hey, I need energy. Justin and Marshall are working me to death at the barn."

He went over to the sink and washed his hands, then joined Nova at the table as Aunt Jean set a plate of pancakes in front of him. Based on his carefree demeanor, Nova figured he was also clueless about her recent traveling. That didn't make sense. She could understand Aunt Jean not remembering because she'd been dead in that timeline. But how could *he* not know?

"I believe that makes twelve so far this morning," Aunt Jean said.

"I'm a growing boy. And since I ate the first batch at six this morning, I don't think you can count those." He smiled and shoved a huge bite in his mouth before turning his attention to Nova. "I hear you're finally getting on a horse this morning."

"Yeah, I guess so," Nova answered, still hoping she'd find a way to get out of it. Maybe she'd tell her dad about traveling. He'd want her to stay and talk about it. She glanced at her aunt, who shot Nova a warning look, clearly not wanting her to bring it up right now.

"Don't worry, firefly. Justin knows you've never ridden. I saw him saddling up Marilyn. She's a sweetheart."

"Marilyn? That's her name?"

"Marilyn Monroe." He laughed.

"Oh, you'll love her," Aunt Jean chimed in. "She doesn't like to do anything but walk. I think her third foal wore her out."

"Kids will do that." Dayton winked at Nova.

"Gee, thanks, Dad. And why were you at the barn so early?"

"Justin needed help fixing the paddock gate and a few sections of fence. He wanted to have it done before Marshall showed up this morning."

"C'mon, Nova!" Marshall called from outside.

Nova swung her legs over the bench and looked out the screen door. He was standing on the path to the barn, his hands on his hips. She still wasn't sure about following through with this, but there was only so big a coward she wanted to be. She took her plate to the sink to rinse off, but Aunt Jean took it from her.

"Let me do that, honey. You don't want to keep Marilyn waiting."

"Okay." Nova reluctantly handed over her plate.

"I put a pair of boots by the door for you." Aunt Jean seemed pleased with herself.

Nova sat on the stool by the door and pulled on one of the boots, disappointed that it was a perfect fit. How had her aunt managed that? Had she crept into Nova's room during the night and measured her feet?

Aunt Jean was watching, a knowing look on her face. "I have magic powers." She winked at Nova and went back to rinsing plates.

Nova pulled on the other boot and stood. "How do I look?"

"Like a real rider," Dayton mumbled as he attempted to bolt down another bite of pancakes. Nova could see where her little brother got his table manners.

Marshall was already in the saddle when Nova

arrived at the barn, but Justin was standing, holding the reins of two horses. They were all tacked up and ready to go. One of the horses was a tall, muscular chestnut, his coat nearly matching Justin's hair. He was pawing impatiently at the ground. The other horse stood quietly, her gentle eyes framed by a long, blond mane. Her tail was also blond, but her coat was the color of spun gold.

"This is Connie's horse, Marilyn," Justin said. "She's as gentle as they come. Connie doesn't like to do much but trail ride, and that suits this girl just fine."

"It suits me too," agreed Nova. "She's beautiful. I see why you named her Marilyn."

Justin laughed. "That was Connie's idea. She said she was as pretty as Marilyn Monroe."

Justin showed Nova how to mount, and she swung her leg over with ease. Marilyn stood patiently while Nova settled herself in the saddle. Maybe this wouldn't be so bad after all, she thought. Justin took the lead on his horse with Marshall behind him on Bo. As soon as the other two horses began walking, Marilyn stepped in behind them without waiting for Nova to figure out what to do. They crossed the field beyond the riding ring, then followed a well-worn trail into the woods. The ground was packed down solidly except for an occasional tree root that had somehow managed to break through. Marilyn seemed to know exactly where to step to avoid them. After a few minutes, Nova relaxed a little and allowed herself to enjoy the scenery.

The trees formed a dense canopy, blocking out much of the sun and making the temperature drop a few degrees. As they moved along, sunlight broke through in places in a burst of brilliant color as it reflected off of the dew on the leaves. It was as if they had ridden into an enchanted forest. Flowers sprung up here and there along the trail, especially in the places where sunlight reached the ground. The purple, yellow, and white wildflowers weren't like the ones that grew in Aunt Jean's garden behind the house, but they were every bit as beautiful.

After ten or fifteen minutes, the trail opened into a small glade where the flowers that grew along the path bloomed in abundance.

The sudden burst of color made Nova gasp. "This is incredible!"

Justin looked over his shoulder and smiled. "Takes your breath away, doesn't it? Personally, this is the kind of garden I like. But don't tell Aunt Jean I said so. She loves her garden behind the house."

"I think I like this better too. It's beautiful."

It didn't matter that the flowers had overtaken the path, because the horses obviously knew the way and continued moving forward until they reached the trail opening on the other side. Nova looked back to take in the scene again as they entered the woods. After the brilliant light and color of the glade, the forest seemed darker. Nova wondered what kind of animals inhabited the woods.

Marshall looked back at her. "Kinda spooky, isn't it? Justin says there are foxes, bobcats, and coyotes around here sometimes. It's okay if you're scared."

Nova felt a chill go up her spine. "I don't think it's scary," she lied.

"Oh." He seemed disappointed.

"Besides, I have you to take care of me, right?"

He brightened. "Yeah! I know what to do if we see one."

Justin hiked one leg over the front of his saddle and looked back. "Mostly you see deer and squirrels."

"But there *are* the dangerous animals too, right?" Marshall insisted.

"Sure, there are, big guy." Justin winked at Nova. "But you leave them alone and they'll leave you alone."

Justin turned back to face forward. As he did, he rubbed his horse's neck, talking to him. "That's a good boy, Sonny," he said affectionately.

Nova envied his ease with his horse and made a conscious effort to relax the rigid muscles in her back and shoulders. She felt a little foolish now for being such a coward and imagined Alana in her place. Nothing frightened her. The scene at the pool played in her head again—five-year-old Allie standing by the water. *"Come on, Nova! Jump in!"* Nova smiled.

"Okay, Allie," she muttered under her breath. She cautiously patted Marilyn's neck.

The mare tossed her head slightly, as if to thank her for the gesture. Nova leaned all the way forward and laid her head against the mare's neck. Marilyn continued along the path as if it were perfectly natural.

"Look at you!" Justin said approvingly.

Nova sat up and grinned. Maybe she'd take a few lessons before they went home after all.

They continued along the trail in what must have been a giant loop because as they broke out of the woods, they could see the barn and house across the field. Nova was surprised by how disappointed she was that their ride was coming to an end.

When Justin helped her down, she said sincerely, "I hope you'll take me with you again."

"You bet," he said, smiling. "So what do you think about horses now?"

"I think I might want to take Marilyn home with me," she replied in earnest.

Justin laughed. "I'm afraid Connie would have something to say about that. Sonny's my horse. He's won the Connecticut Championship Steeplechase two years in a row and took reserve champion in the nationals last year."

"That's amazing!" Nova had never even heard of steeplechasing before coming to Willow Hill but had since learned that it was a harrowing race across a course heavy with seemingly impossible obstacles. It wasn't a sport for the faint of heart.

Sonny pawed the ground impatiently, and Justin patted him on the neck. "This guy's ready for his workout. He doesn't enjoy walking the trails as much as we do."

"He's beautiful," Nova said before turning her attention back to Marilyn. "She's my favorite though."

The mare nuzzled Nova's shoulder, and Nova patted her neck again.

"You can ride her any time you like. Connie hasn't been able to ride since about her fifth month."

Marshall was apparently anxious to do something other than stand there talking. "You can go back to the house if you want to, Nova. Justin and me can take care of the horses."

Justin nodded and winked.

"Okay, kiddo. I'll go back to the house."

Justin took Marilyn's reins, and Nova walked up the hill. She met her dad, who was headed back to the barn.

"How was it, firefly?"

"Great," she said. "Not nearly as hard as I thought it would be. And Marilyn was wonderful."

"That's good, but I guess you'll be asking for a horse now too." He laughed as he continued down the path.

Nova headed up toward the house again, content to be alone with her thoughts. When she stepped through the door to the kitchen, Aunt Jean was nowhere to be seen. The clock on the wall read just after ten o'clock. That gave her a couple of hours to relax and think about her next move before she'd be expected downstairs again. Lunch was at noon. No matter what else was going on, no one missed a meal in this house.

Nova kicked off her boots, suddenly worn out. If a trail ride made her this tired, she couldn't imagine how Marshall was able to spend the whole day at the barn without collapsing. Nine-year-old boys must have boundless energy. At least her little brother did. It was one of the things she'd missed the most about him.

After she'd showered and changed clothes, she lay

down on the four-poster and enjoyed the pleasantly cool breeze that drifted in through the open window. North Carolina could be hot and humid in the summer, but the weather had been mild since their arrival, with daytime temperatures barely hitting the upper seventies before dipping into the low sixties at night. Aunt Jean had joked that they must have brought Connecticut weather down with them. The house was air-conditioned of course, but because of the unseasonably cool weather, they'd had the windows open every day.

The birds were twittering the garden. Somewhere off in the distance came the faint sound of a tractor.

"You're right, Aunt Jean," she mumbled sleepily. "You're not in the country if you can't hear one…"

Nova closed her eyes and let herself slip into a half sleep. In that state, she felt the connection to the tapestry. It wasn't intrusive. It was more like a gentle hold—a delicate hand laid softly on her arm. It was strange that she could still feel it, but she wasn't particularly uneasy about that fact anymore. If it was going to pull her back in, it would've done it already.

Nova took a deep breath and let it out, totally relaxed. "I know you're there."

Talking to the tapestry didn't seem odd at all. On the contrary, she found it comforting. Alana was there, in some of Nova's timelines. Nova could imagine her tapping her foot and saying, "Let's get this show on the road, little sister. I have things I want to do!"

"I'm coming soon," Nova whispered.

She felt as if her body was beginning to float very slightly above the quilt that covered the bed. It was a familiar sensation. Instead of transitioning to the next level, she stayed there, hovering, pleased with her newfound control. If someone were to walk into her room, would they see her levitating above the bed? Or was this feeling totally in her mind? That question would bear exploring later on. Right now, all she wanted to do was to stay there, hovering between worlds. She wasn't ready to make a move, but feeling the closeness of the tapestry made her feel less disconnected from her sister.

Another breeze floated in from the window and brushed across her face, breaking the spell and returning her to her present reality. Nova sat up and rubbed her eyes. Maybe it wasn't a good idea to flirt with the tapestry until she was ready to go inside again. At some point, the temptation to go back would be too strong, and she couldn't afford to make another mistake. She'd been lucky to get this chance to start over. It wouldn't necessarily work out if she screwed up again. No, the next time she traveled, she'd have to make sure her plan was perfect.

Nova picked up the phone to call Ethan. Hearing his voice always grounded her. He had a way of making her feel as though everything would work out. After several rings, the answering machine picked up. Disappointed, Nova tried again with the same result. She hung up without leaving a message.

CHAPTER 5

Sometime before noon, Dayton tapped on her door and stepped inside. He was wearing jeans and a white dress shirt, and his normal boyish attitude was decidedly missing.

"Jason called," he said as if that was the worst thing that could happen. "He reminded me that I have three book signings this week in New York. I have to be there tonight." He clearly had no desire to go.

Nova shook herself awake. "That's part of being a famous author."

He closed the door and lowered his voice. "Yeah, sure. Except I had no idea I'd agreed to do this, and one of the books I'm signing is one I've never seen before. I mean, it's totally unfamiliar. How is that even possible? I came up with something in this life I'd never even thought of before?"

"I guess something happened in this reality that gave you the idea. Nothing about it seems familiar?"

"Not a thing. I'll have to speed-read it on the plane."

"Yikes."

"Yeah. Jason wanted to know what chapter I plan to do at the reading." He plopped down on the armchair in the corner. "Your mother's going with me. We're leaving for the airport in ten minutes. She wants to shop for the baby in New York. I shudder to think what that'll cost me."

"She's really into it, isn't she? The baby, I mean."

"That's an understatement. She'll bankrupt us when

you and Marshall start having kids."

"And Alana."

"Oh… right." He looked as if he wanted to say something else but thought better of it. "Will you be okay here with just Marshall and Aunt Jean for a few days?"

"Of course. There's Justin and Connie too."

"I know." He stood and started for the door but stopped and looked back. "Promise you won't do anything while I'm gone. You know what I mean."

It was too late to make that promise since she'd already traveled from this timeline once and come back. But she couldn't tell him that. Not now anyway.

"I won't." Another lie. Nova wondered how many she'd told since he died on the bridge.

He opened the door just in time for Celeste to come running in. She was stunning in a black skirt, plum-colored silk blouse, and black heels. Nova's mind flashed back to her mother sitting at the kitchen table, circling want ads, the orange streak in her hair.

"You look great, Mom," she said.

"Thanks, honey. If I do, it's a miracle! Did your dad tell you?" Her mother was nearly breathless. "I barely had time to pack. We'll have to go meet Jason straight from the airport. Honestly, Day, how do you forget book signings in New York?"

"Babe, I told you. He must have changed the dates." Her dad looked flustered.

"I know. I know. But you'd forget your head if it wasn't attached." Celeste kissed Nova's forehead. "I made an appointment for you to have your stitches removed in Charlotte. I wrote it all down for your aunt."

"Yuck." Nova grimaced.

"Oh, don't worry. It won't hurt." Celeste tried to give what she obviously thought was a reassuring smile, but Nova wasn't buying it. "And take care of Marshall, okay? I don't want to come back and find out he tried to jump a fence on that horse and split his head open."

"He'll be fine," Nova said quickly. "I won't let him do anything crazy. And you know Justin won't either."

"I know, honey. Just being a worrying mother, I guess." She sat on the bed beside Nova. "Honestly, I think you and Aunt Jean could handle a house full of kids, so one little boy should be no trouble."

Nova smiled. "Sure. Just have a great time in New York."

"Thanks, honey. I'll bring you back something from Bloomingdale's." She was beaming. Trips to New York were just about her favorite thing. "Come on, Day. If we miss our flight, Jason will have a fit."

She exited the room as quickly as she'd come in, Dayton right behind her. Nova listened to her parents talking down the hall. Her mother was complaining that she hadn't brought the proper clothes for a trip to "the city" and that she'd most likely have to buy something when they got there. Nova shook her head, thinking about her dad's comment. Their trip was going to cost him a fortune.

A few minutes later, Dayton stuck his head in the door again. "Don't do any shopping while we're gone. I think your mother has that covered."

He didn't really seem upset anymore. Maybe he was appreciating the fact that some things didn't change, no matter what timeline he was in. Dayton Grant loved his wife and enjoyed seeing her happy. If he could have given her the moon, he would have. It was no wonder that Celeste had fallen into depression after his death. Nova vowed to make sure that never happened again.

"Everything will be okay, Dad." She smiled reassuringly. "Have fun in New York."

"Will do, firefly." And with that, he was out the door.

Nova sat on the window seat until she heard her parents descend the stairs and close the massive front door. The house was instantly quiet, except for the outdoor sounds.

She thought about climbing back on the bed and trying to feel the tapestry again, but there was no way she'd be able to relax after all the commotion.

A wonderful aroma wafted in from the hall. Aunt Jean was baking something that smelled delicious. Deciding to check it out, she hurried down the stairs. It was lunchtime anyway, and she was starving.

The kitchen table was loaded down with sandwiches, potato salad, strawberries, and pies. Her aunt always made sure there were baked goods in the house. *It must be a Southern thing.*

Nova took in the wonderful smell of freshly baked apple pies. "Did I mention that we're gonna weigh a ton when we leave here, Aunt Jean?"

Her aunt was pulling another pie out of the oven. This one had a meringue topping. She gave Nova an appreciative smile. "I guess I just love baking, especially when I have family around."

"Don't stop on my account." Nova laughed. "I'm spoiled now. Is that chocolate cream pie?"

"Yes, it is. Your favorite, right?"

"Absolutely! We mostly have store-bought pies and cookies at home, and it's pretty rare that we even have those. Mom's kind of a health nut."

"I noticed that." Aunt Jean laughed. "But between you and me, she took a huge slice of apple pie with her to eat on the plane."

A large covered pot was simmering on the stovetop. She walked over and turned the flame down a little.

"What's that?" Nova couldn't imagine needing more food than the spread already laid out.

"It's beef stew. That's for dinner tonight." She motioned for Nova to sit. "It's better if it cooks slowly all day."

The plates were already on the table, so Nova plopped down in her usual spot, grabbed a turkey sandwich from the tray, and took a big bite. Her aunt sat across from her, suddenly serious. Nova had another bite chewed and swallowed before she caught her aunt studying her.

"Is everything okay, Aunt Jean?"

"Everything's fine. I want you to tell me more about the timeline with Alana."

Nova put her partially eaten turkey sandwich back on the plate. "What about the others? Won't they be in soon? It's lunchtime."

"I took food down to them at the barn before you came in. They're eating in the apartment with Connie. She didn't feel like walking up to the house."

"So all this food is for you and me?"

"I made extra." That was clearly all she planned to say about it.

"Oh," Nova said. Why was her aunt being so mysterious?

Her aunt had one topic on her mind, and there was clearly no getting her off of it. She leaned forward, her arms on the table. "I was wondering, did you talk to your dad before coming back here? Back to this timeline? Did he know you were traveling again?"

Nova quickly swallowed another bite of sandwich. "No. I decided to do that on my own. I only told Ethan."

"Ethan? You talked to Ethan but not your dad?"

"Dad wanted to go back to talk to Grandma Kate again. I didn't see the point, so I decided to go ahead and do it. Neither of us wanted to stay there even though it meant that, for now, Alana…" Nova couldn't bear to finish the sentence, but she didn't need to.

"Why did he want to go see my sister?" Aunt Jean's riveting eye contact was unnerving.

Feeling a little as if she were on trial, Nova cleared her throat nervously. "He thought she might know what to do. I didn't want to go because seeing her before was pointless. All she did was talk about traveling causing nothing but pain. She kept saying it never worked out the way you wanted it to. Anyway, she refused to help us."

Aunt Jean's face turned red as she set her jaw. "You asked her for help, and she said no?"

"Yeah. I think she was scared to help us. She kept saying that traveling made things worse. I know she lost her first family, but there must have been times she wanted to try again. I don't know why she never did."

"I say we ask her."

Nova felt the hairs stand up on the back of her neck again. "You mean go back and ask her?"

Was Aunt Jean suggesting one or both of them travel back to when her grandmother was alive? Nova had been a child when she died, so what good would it do for her to visit that time?

Aunt Jean's expression changed to one of confusion. "Why would we have to travel?"

It was Nova's turn to be confused. How could they ask her dead grandmother anything now?

Before she could ask that question, Marshall burst in the back door. "Hey, Nova! You should come back to the barn. We're gonna build jumps out in the field this afternoon. Justin says they're training some of the horses for a steeplechase and they need new jumps."

"I'm pretty tired, Marsh. Besides, I saw a bunch of jumps out there before," Nova said.

"Yeah, but the horses have seen those too many times. Justin says we need to surprise them with new ones so they don't freak out when they go somewhere else and see all new jumps. It's gonna be really fun! We're gonna have barrels and tree limbs and all kinds of stuff."

Aunt Jean nudged Nova. "You go help him, honey. We'll talk later."

She carried their plates to the counter, clearly through talking for now. Nova was disappointed but tried to be enthusiastic for Marshall's sake. She couldn't get her aunt's comment out of her head though. If she wasn't going to travel, how did Aunt Jean plan to talk to her dead sister?

CHAPTER 6

Nova helped Justin and Marshall build jumps until midafternoon. They dragged large limbs from the woods to the barn. Justin trimmed them and smoothed out the rough places before placing them in a pile and tying them together with twine. Next, they took an old door from the barn and leaned it against bales of hay with flowerpots full of yellow blooms on top. Justin even came up with the idea to build a jump from old tires stacked on top of each other. Around three thirty, he drove into town to get some used tires from a body shop two blocks off of the main street.

Before he left, he pulled his pickup truck around to the front of the barn and called Marshall over. "I want you to sweep out the brick walkway while I'm gone. If you finish that, you can start rinsing out the water buckets. Okay, big guy?"

"Sure, I can do that." Marshall beamed. "You want me to do anything else? I can wash Bo."

Justin's face took on a serious expression. "I don't want you washing Bo while I'm not here. I only want you to do these two things: sweep the barn and rinse the buckets. If you finish all that, go back to the house or go up to the apartment with Connie, all right?"

"Okay." Marshall kicked the ground with his shoe. "I'm not five, you know."

Justin reached out of the truck window and gave him

a playful punch in the jaw. "Yeah, I know."

Marshall jumped backward, laughing.

Justin's gonna make a great dad, Nova thought as he drove away.

Marshall took off for the barn and was already pushing the wide broom up the aisle when she stepped through the open double doors. She sat on a bench outside Marilyn's stall and watched her little brother sweep the large expanse of brick walkway, amazed at his transformation from the little kid who played video games, rode his skateboard, and whined about being bored, to this determined young man who thought sweeping the barn and mucking out stalls was the best thing ever.

He was completely focused on his task, making sure he swept away every single bit of straw, grass, and dirt. Every few minutes, he leaned over and picked up a stubborn piece of debris, walked over to the entrance, and tossed it outside. Then he picked up the broom again and continued sweeping. After twenty minutes, he had barely made it halfway up the aisle.

"We won't be eating off that brick, you know, kiddo."

Marshall ignored her and continued his uncharacteristically meticulous efforts. Nova figured he was going out of his way to show Justin he could handle taking care of the barn without anyone looking over his shoulder. With that thought, she decided to go back to the house for a little while. Justin hadn't asked her to stay, and she wanted to talk to Aunt Jean.

"I'll be back in a little while, okay?" she asked.

Marshall's expression said it all. He was delighted she was leaving. "Sure! I'll handle things here. You don't need to stay and watch me."

"Okay. Just remember what Justin said."

Marshall rolled his eyes. "Duh."

Nova headed up to the house, resisting the urge to look over her shoulder. She didn't want him to think she didn't trust him, but she knew her little brother. He had a talent for getting into trouble, and there were probably hundreds of ways he could get hurt in a barn full of horses and farm equipment. The fact that she could travel back to undo an accident did little to mute her concerns. Still, Justin trusted him enough to leave him there, so the least she could do was give Marshall the benefit of the doubt.

When she came in the back door, the kitchen was empty, but something was in the oven and the pot was still on the stove with the flame on low. As usual, the kitchen was filled with a wonderful aroma. She stepped out onto the veranda and looked around. No Aunt Jean.

Disappointed, Nova figured she should go back to the barn to keep an eye on Marshall, but as she opened the back door and stepped outside, she noticed Justin's truck coming up the driveway. Marshall ran out to greet him, still hauling the broom. She watched Justin get out of the truck and head into the barn with him. Relieved, she headed upstairs to her room instead.

A cleaning crew was working in the front hall and both front rooms. Two women were busily dusting the furniture, baseboards, and molding while a young man stood precariously on a ladder, cleaning the crystal chandelier in the dining room. Nova had never seen anyone working in the house, but it made sense that her aunt couldn't keep up with everything that needed to be done in a place like this.

A young woman was on her hands and knees, cleaning the wood floor just off the kitchen. When Nova approached, she looked up and smiled. Nova stepped around her, careful to walk on the floor that was dry.

"Umm... have you seen my aunt?"

"She went into town earlier to pick something up. I think you have more company coming."

"More company? Who?"

"I don't know, miss."

"When did she say she'd be back?"

"She didn't say, miss."

"Okay." Nova stood there awkwardly. It seemed rude to just walk away, but she didn't want to stand over her either. She cleared her throat. "My aunt made sandwiches earlier. I'm sure she saved them. Would you like one?"

"We had them earlier, miss. Your aunt is always so thoughtful!"

"Okay." That explained the extra food at lunch. "Well…"

Nova couldn't think of anything else to say. Besides, it bothered her that the girl, who appeared to be no more than a teenager, kept calling her "miss." So Nova headed up the stairs to her room. Maybe Uncle Bill's son, Michael, and his family were coming. They were the only ones she could think of. If there were suddenly more kids in the house, it would be hard to get any time alone with her aunt. Maybe they'd meet for another late-night hot chocolate.

Nova had worked up a sweat working on the jumps, so she bathed again quickly and changed into shorts and a white tee shirt. With nothing else to do, she sat on the window seat and admired the view.

Willow Hill had to be the most beautiful place on earth. She was beginning to feel as much at home here as she did at their house in Connecticut. But it was more than just feeling at home. This place was magical, especially her room, with its tranquil blue walls, armchair, cozy four-poster bed, and the window seat overlooking the garden that her aunt had lovingly planted and tended to for years. That first day at Willow Hill, Aunt Jean had told Nova that this was the most peaceful room in the house, a place to get in touch with your thoughts. That had certainly proven to be true.

Nova climbed onto the four-poster and lay down, gazing at the beadboard ceiling. This was becoming a pattern. Every time she found herself with a little free time, she ended up on the bed in her room, staring at the ceiling. There were plenty of other things to do at Willow Hill. She could go back to the barn and help out or explore the attic some more. Who knew what she'd find if she really turned that space inside out. There could be other paintings of people her family had erased from existence. She shivered over that morbid thought.

The sprawling house had plenty of other rooms to explore—rooms she'd never seen. Maybe she'd even find the elusive clock. She could hear it now. The daytime sounds coming from the open window drowned it out somewhat, but there it was. Tick... tock...

In spite of the plethora of other activities available to her, she continued to lie there, staring at the ceiling and imagining a life with both of her siblings. Marshall would probably drive Alana crazy. They were so similar. Putting them together would be like putting a match to a stick of dynamite. Sooner or later there was bound to be an explosion. And yet, Alana would understand their little brother in a way Nova had never been able to. Maybe they'd actually be best buddies—partners in crime. *If that happens, God help us!* Nova smiled.

After a while, she closed her eyes and felt it again, the gentle tug of the tapestry. She let herself be drawn in... just a little. It wasn't hard to stop it, to stay in exactly the same spot. She was in control, not yet to the place where her body began to feel the floating sensation.

She remained in that state, listening to the birds outside, trying to ignore the clock. It was funny that she'd never before noticed the ticking during the day. Maybe there wasn't a clock at all. Maybe the ticking was in her imagination, triggered any time she was on the verge of traveling—a way for her mind to latch on to a target. Nova tried to no avail to block it out by concentrating on the sounds drifting in from outside. She could still hear it growing louder and louder in her brain. Tick... tock...

There was no denying that she wanted to see the tapestry again. What would be the harm? She'd be careful not to connect with another life, but only look inside it to see what could be. Tick… tock…

Nova felt her body float as if adrift in a raft as the ocean gradually rose and fell. The sensation was pleasant, comforting. She lingered there, enjoying the feeling and marveling at her newfound control. She allowed herself to be drawn into the tunnel where visions bombarded her. She pushed them away as before and found herself in total darkness. The tapestry was just ahead, beyond this void. In spite of that knowledge, the familiar panic threatened to overtake her. What if this time she was really lost, floating blindly in a vast black pool? What if she'd only found it before by accident? Nova strained to see ahead, but saw nothing.

She had no idea how much time passed. Had it taken this long the last time? She struggled to regain the calmness she'd felt as she floated, but it eluded her. Her head hurt, just as it had the previous time. Nova had forgotten about that particular side effect but found it oddly comforting that her previous experience was repeating itself. She struggled to see behind the black curtain that blotted out everything around her. There was still no silver cloud in the distance. Maybe she was going in the wrong direction, if there even was such a thing.

Her headache subsided as quickly as it had come on. Nova stared intently ahead, and then there it was, just as suddenly as it had appeared the first time. Relief washed over her like a cold shower, all panic forgotten. The glimmering silver cloud unfolded in all its brilliance. If anything, it seemed more magnificent than before.

She allowed herself to be pulled in. It required no effort on her part, as if she were tethered by an invisible rope to some point deep inside the web. In spite of the fact that she seemed to be caught like a fish on a line, she didn't feel threatened and had the sense that she could break free if she really wanted to.

She gazed around as she entered the shimmering network of intricately woven timelines. They no longer seemed like an elaborate spider web created in a predetermined pattern. There was no symmetry to this place. Threads wove in and out of each other, sometimes shooting off in one direction only to stop abruptly or change direction entirely. It was a gloriously stunning mess. Nova thought of Ethan's room. *He'd love it here.* He was, in his own way, a gloriously stunning mess.

With that thought still fluttering around in her brain, Nova moved deeper into the tapestry. Countless glowing timelines were laid out before her. She could have spent a lifetime peering into them and still not seen them all. It was overwhelming. She drifted farther and farther in, but there were always more ahead of her.

Slowly, she began to worry that she was going too far. She looked around and realized that something was different, not that there would have ever been a way to memorize this place. Still, she had the feeling deep in her core that the tapestry had changed, but she couldn't put her finger on exactly what was different. Some of her threads glowed a bright blue, but others seemed to be emitting a paler light. Could that be it? Maybe she simply hadn't noticed the variance before because she'd been awestruck by the brilliance of the place.

She touched one of the timelines whose light was less brilliant and saw herself walking down the hallway at school. By the look on her face, Nova could tell that this was not a happy timeline. She knew instinctively which it was. It was the one without her dad.

Nova pulled back from that life, but now it glowed with a fresh luminance, as if touching it had given it a boost of power. She found that thought frightening. Had she inadvertently given that reality a fighting chance? Why else would it now be as vivid as the others?

Nova shook off the thought and touched another

timeline. She was, once again, in Europe with her dad. Only at this spot in the timeline, they were obviously in Paris, the two of them sitting on a bench and watching pedestrians breeze in and out of the shops that bordered the street. Celeste and Alana exited a boutique directly across from them, carrying bags loaded down with whatever they had found inside that they couldn't live without. Apparently her mom had found her other shopping half in Alana. Nova smiled as she watched them chattering excitedly about their purchases. *So, this is what a Paris trip would have looked like.*

As Nova took in the scene, she felt that reality tugging, trying to draw her all the way in. She'd be in Paris with her sister. It would be wonderful—a trip to remember her whole life. She felt herself bonding with that life. It would be so easy…

No! With some effort, she pulled back, reminding herself to be more careful. She couldn't forget why she was here, why the only reality that mattered was the one she was searching for. There would be other trips. And if there weren't, so be it. She'd be happy as long as she had her whole family.

She resumed her search. As she visited other strands, other versions of her life, she noticed that they were all ones she hadn't seen when she was there before. Even with so many to choose from, that struck her as odd. She looked around at her other threads weaving in and out around her and couldn't shake the feeling that it was all *different.* None of the patterns seemed familiar. It was as if she were seeing it all for the first time again. But how could she feel that when she couldn't possibly map a place like this out in her brain? And yet even though she'd come in just like before, she was seeing none of the same timelines.

An unsettled feeling grew inside her, a sense that she should get out of there or something bad would happen. Gripped by fear, Nova realized that she didn't know how to get back. When she'd been in the tapestry before, she'd left through a timeline. How could she have been so stupid not to realize that she wouldn't know how to return to her room at Willow Hill?

If there was a way in, there had to be a way out. Nova searched her surroundings frantically for an obvious opening. She wanted to scream for help, but who would hear her in this place between realities? She touched other strands, hoping to find the first one she'd visited. Maybe from there, she'd be able to remember the way. Each one she touched showed her a different life, but none were the ones she was looking for. In fact, there were no repeats at all, almost as if they changed the instant she left them. Or perhaps she was simply lost in this maze of countless glowing strands.

The terrifying possibility that she would never get back took hold of her and wouldn't let go. Nova stopped trying to find a familiar strand and flew from lifetime to lifetime, trying to find one that would take her home or to Willow Hill. Anywhere but imprisoned in the tapestry.

She was exhausted. Weakly, she touched a faint thread and saw herself as a small child, sitting in a church pew with her parents on either side. They were waiting for the service to start, and she was already restless. Her mother leaned down and whispered, "Be still, Nova."

Nova pulled back. "Be still, Nova," she whispered, startled that she could actually hear her voice. It hadn't dawned on her that she'd have the ability to speak out loud while in the tapestry. "Be still. Be still."

She closed her eyes and cleared her mind. Almost instantly, she felt another force pulling at her gently. It was as if a hand had reached out to help her fight the tether dragging her deep into the tapestry. She focused on this new force and felt herself being pulled along through the maze of timelines. Part of her feared that she was actually being transported deeper inside the tapestry, but she had no choice but to let it take her. She was too weak to fight it.

It seemed only seconds passed before she was in the void again. Looking back, she saw the silver cloud retreating into the darkness until it was no longer visible. And then she was back—back on the four-poster in her room at Willow Hill.

Nova sat bolt upright, struggling to catch her breath from a massive adrenaline rush. Her shirt was damp from perspiration. She crawled to the end of the bed and gripped one of the posts. The room seemed to rock slightly as she hung on. Several minutes passed before the room settled down and she trusted herself to stand.

As soon as her bare feet hit the cool wood floor, she felt better. She tiptoed into the bathroom and filled the tub. This would be her third bath in the same day, but she didn't care. After shedding her damp clothes, she lowered herself into the warm water, leaned her head back, and closed her eyes. Slowly the tension left her muscles, but her brain was still reeling.

That was the second time she'd stupidly dived in without thinking, and the repercussions could have been devastating. Clearly, she wasn't ready to take matters into her own hands since she apparently couldn't tell the difference between a good idea and a really bad one.

As the water cooled, she made a decision. She dried off, dressed, and headed downstairs to find Aunt Jean. She'd dodged a bullet… again. It had been foolish to think she had control over this formidable power. From now on, she'd talk to her aunt first.

She was surprised to, once again, step into an empty kitchen. The oven was still on, and when she lifted the lid of the heavy pot simmering on the stove, the delicious aroma of beef stew filled the air.

She set the lid in place and called, "Aunt Jean?"

The house was eerily quiet. The cleaning crew had left, and Marshall was apparently still at the barn. But where was her aunt? She took a ladle from the drawer and stirred the stew. It smelled heavenly. She replaced the lid again and stepped out onto the veranda. The scent of flowers dwarfed the smells coming from the kitchen. Nova started to sit in one of the cushioned chairs to wait for Aunt Jean, but changed her mind and wandered out into the garden instead.

As she strolled along the path, she heard voices coming from the gazebo. Her heart sank. Maybe the "company" was here. Nova felt guilty for dreading their arrival. It wasn't fair for her to expect to have Aunt Jean all to herself. Still, she had so much she wanted to talk to her about, and having Michael's family around would make that nearly impossible. She studied the stone path as she shuffled along, engulfed in her thoughts until she nearly ran into the gazebo steps.

She looked up and saw Aunt Jean in one of the wicker chairs, watching Nova with an amused smile. Sitting across from her, in a blue checked dress with little red strawberries embroidered along the hem, was a very-much-alive Grandma Kate.

CHAPTER 7

The two women ceased their conversation and waited for her to say something, but Nova didn't seem able to do anything but stare at her grandmother with her mouth hanging open. Aunt Jean would surely point out any minute that she was going to catch a fly.

"It's nice to see you, Nova." Grandma Kate smiled warmly.

"You're supposed to be dead," Nova blurted out before she could stop herself.

Her aunt and grandmother exchanged looks, then burst out laughing.

"Well, that's quite a greeting!" Aunt Jean managed to get out. She looked at her sister. "Did you know you were supposed to be dead?"

"This is the first I'm hearing about it, Jeannie." Kate chuckled.

Nova was mortified. "I'm sorry! It's just... in this timeline..." She had no idea how to finish.

The realization hit her squarely in the pit of her stomach. This was not the same timeline she'd left when she'd brought Alana back. Because in that timeline, Grandma Kate had been dead for years. So if this wasn't the same timeline, what other differences would there be? She did a quick mental inventory of everyone since she'd come back.

They were all here except for Alana. So, that much was the same. Ethan had been exactly the same when she'd talked to him on the phone, remembering their time together exactly as Nova remembered it. So, maybe that part of her life was the same too. But other things would certainly be different. There couldn't be just this one thing. Because this one thing was her grandmother not being dead anymore. A change like that had to have ripple effects.

"Come sit down, honey." Aunt Jean motioned for Nova to join them. As soon as she'd sat down, her aunt leaned forward. "Now why don't you tell us why you thought Kate was dead?"

Nova stared at her hands clasped in her lap like two fists molded together. Her knuckles were turning white. "I just thought…" She looked at her grandmother. "I thought I was in another timeline."

Kate's eyes grew wide. "What do you mean? Have you been traveling?" Her eyes darted toward her sister. "Jeannie, what have you done?"

"Oh, don't start that! You know perfectly well I've been talking to Nova about traveling."

"Well, it sounds more like she's doing it on her own. If that's not the case, then explain it to me."

"Grandma," Nova jumped in, "she didn't know I was going to travel. I did that without telling her. And now I think I've really messed up. I'm not where I thought I was. But this looked like the right one when I was in the tapestry—"

"The tapestry?" Kate interrupted. "Good Lord! What were you doing there?"

"I was trying to get back to my old timeline—the one with Marshall."

"What on earth are you talking about?"

Aunt Jean put her hand on her sister's arm. "Calm down. Let her explain."

"This is all wrong." Nova moaned. She was suddenly light-headed. "I'm glad you're alive, Grandma. I just…"

"You don't know where you are?" her grandmother asked solemnly.

"I guess... yes." Nova's heart was racing. "I don't know if I messed up before or just now. I was upstairs, and I went back to the tapestry. Is that why I'm in a different timeline? Did it just happen? Oh my God... what about Ethan? I talked to him last night, before I went back! Have I messed that up too? I need to call him!"

Aunt Jean gripped Nova's arm. "Child, listen to me. I'm going to tell you about last night and this morning, and you tell me if it's what you remember too."

"Okay." Nova's voice was shaky.

"I found you in Marshall's room. We had cocoa in the kitchen, and you told me about bringing Alana back."

"That's what I remember. Then I helped Marshall and Justin put new jumps together."

Aunt Jean nodded. "Right."

"When you and I were talking, you said we should ask Grandma Kate why she wouldn't help Dad and me. I didn't understand because she was supposed to be dead."

"I'm right here, you know," Kate spoke up.

Aunt Jean gave her sister a stern look, then turned her attention back to Nova. "It seems to me that you're in the same timeline as you were before you visited the tapestry earlier today—the same one you came back to last night. But it's not the one you thought you were in, apparently."

"I don't understand. I was sure it was the right one. Everything looked exactly the way it did before."

Kate's hands were shoved in her lap, and her lips were pursed, as if she'd tasted something bitter. She clearly didn't like talking about the tapestry.

Nova cleared her throat nervously. "When I touched this timeline, I saw us turning into Willow Hill and moving up the driveway. Aunt Jean, you were standing on the porch waiting for us. You had on a yellow shirt and riding boots, just like the first time. When I moved forward, I saw myself in the attic, looking through the trunks." She decided to leave out the part about finding the painting of Grandma Kate's first family. Her grandmother seemed on edge enough without adding that memory. "*Everything* seemed the same. It doesn't make sense that I'm in a different timeline. Ethan's the same. Marshall's the same. Alana isn't here, so that's the same." She turned her attention to Kate. "The only thing different is you, Grandma."

"I'm glad about that," Kate answered tersely. "Never did fancy the idea of being dead."

"I'm glad too!" Nova's frustration level rose exponentially. "But *why* are you here? Why haven't more things changed because you're alive? I picked this strand because it seemed to be *exactly* the one I was looking for."

Kate sighed. "There's no such thing, I'm afraid."

"What do you mean?" Nova asked.

"Timelines change constantly. Old ones fade away, and new ones are formed. It's always changing. Each time you visit, each time you touch a thread, your interaction with it has repercussions. That's why Mother warned us about it and never mentioned it again." Kate's gaze shifted toward the garden, but she didn't appear to be looking at the flowers. She was somewhere else. Aunt Jean touched her sister's hand, and she snapped back to the present. "I'm sorry. There's something I should tell you." Her eyes filled with tears as she looked at her granddaughter. "You're so like Mother. She wasn't afraid of anything—always taking matters into her own hands, making decisions for all of us. She never wanted us to go into the tapestry because she knew how dangerous it was."

Aunt Jean squeezed her sister's hand. "You've been there too, haven't you?"

Kate wiped her eyes with a handkerchief she had clutched in her lap. "Many, many times."

Aunt Jean was thunderstruck. "Why did you never tell me?"

"I don't know. I was afraid to share what I'd done, I suppose. Especially when I'd been so hateful to you all—taking Dayton and moving away." Kate looked pleadingly at her sister. "I'm so sorry. I should have told you, but I became caught up in the tapestry—visiting it over and over after Dayton left for college. I always managed to come back, but little things had changed. Most of the time, it didn't make any difference. Our lives were the same. But sometimes..." Kate dabbed her eyes again and shook her head. "I saw my little Danny grow up. He became a builder, like his dad. He was so handsome."

Her gaze turned to Nova, her expression filled with utter sadness. "But I always changed back because of Dayton... and you children. I didn't want what I was doing to affect you all. I was in so much pain, feeling Daniel's loss over and over... and my Danny. I finally made the decision to stop."

"I wish you'd talked to me," Aunt Jean said softly.

"I wanted to, but I was afraid of what you'd say."

Nova said, "Grandma, that's why you stayed away from us? You were afraid you'd mess up our lives?"

"Yes. I argued with your dad about poor little Alana. When I said I wouldn't help, I knew he'd never forgive me. By then, I had gone to the tapestry so many times I'd lost count. And no matter how careful I was, every time I traveled through the tapestry, there were subtle changes. I thought staying away would protect you."

"You should have told Dad."

"Maybe so. But I know how powerful the tapestry is, what it's capable of. I didn't want to put that loaded gun in the hands of someone who had already made one disastrous attempt to travel. Besides, all it ever did for me was make me more miserable. I didn't want that for him."

"But cutting us out of your life hurt him too."

"I know it did. I'm sorry."

Nova threw her arms around her grandmother. "It's

okay, Grandma. You're here now. I know Dad will be happy to see you when he gets back."

"I don't know…"

"He will." Nova sat back in her chair again. "And you don't need to be afraid to help, because you're not alone now. We can all put our heads together and figure this out. You can teach me how to use the tapestry, and I can have my whole family together. I know there must be a timeline that has both Alana and Marshall in it."

"If there is, I've never seen it. I hate telling you that, but it's the truth."

"There must be one! And if there isn't, I'll just do what you did. I'll go back and forth!"

"No! Didn't you hear anything I said? That's no way to live your life. It's unbearable. You never feel connected anywhere. It affects all of your relationships. You'd end up all alone, like me. This is the first time I've seen you or my sister in years. I couldn't let myself be content anywhere, so I kept hopping from one timeline to another until I quit entirely. It almost killed me."

"But if that's the only way…"

Kate sighed. "I don't know if there are any timelines that include both your brother and your sister. I just said *I've* never seen one. But I was going back and forth in my own lives, not yours."

"That's it!" Nova exclaimed. "I'll look in Alana's timelines. Or Marshall's."

Kate nearly jumped out of her chair. "You can't look in anyone's timelines but your own. If you try, it's incredibly painful!"

"I don't care," Nova answered, frowning. "With all I've already been through, I can handle it."

Kate shook her head, her expression stern. "You misunderstand. It's not that it's emotionally painful, although that would be true. It's *physically* painful. You can't get into someone else's timeline. It won't let you. And if you try…

well, imagine grabbing a live power line. If you manage to survive it, you never want to do it again."

Aunt Jean studied Kate for a moment. "Are you speaking from experience?"

Kate looked back and forth between her sister and granddaughter, then solemnly nodded. "I am. Trust me."

"Okay, then teach me about the tapestry," Nova insisted. "Tell me everything you know."

Aunt Jean spoke up. "Hold on, you two. Let's think about this."

"There's nothing to think about! I'm going back in no matter what anyone says. I'm not gonna give up!"

"No one is telling you to give up, honey. But let me point out that you've rushed into your newfound power without thinking a couple of times already. How did that turn out for you?" Aunt Jean's voice softened. "Let's put all our heads together this time and have a real plan before jumping in. Agreed?"

Kate twisted the handkerchief into a rope while shaking her head vigorously.

Aunt Jean frowned at her sister. "Kate, what's the point of having this power to change your life if you don't use it for something like this? We're not talking about getting more money or more possessions. We're talking about your own granddaughter. God didn't give us this gift so we'd be afraid of it."

Kate gazed into the garden at nothing in particular. She seemed far away. "Maybe that's always been my problem. I've been afraid for so long."

"You don't need to be now," Nova said. "You have us."

Aunt Jean patted Kate's arm, smiling. "That settles it. Now let's get something to eat before we all waste away. Besides, I have a surprise for you."

"You know I hate surprises," Kate muttered.

"Maybe you won't hate this one." Aunt Jean chuckled

as they walked back to the house.

CHAPTER 8

After dinner, Marshall took off for the barn again while Kate, Aunt Jean, and Nova cleaned up. Aunt Jean spooned the leftover stew into a glass bowl, covered it with foil, and placed it in the refrigerator. She didn't speak for at least ten minutes, which Nova figured had to be a record for her aunt. Something was clearly on her mind.

Finally, her aunt turned her attention to Kate and cleared her throat. "What did you think of Justin?"

Kate rinsed the last dish and placed it in the dishwasher. "He's a nice young man. He and Connie are a cute couple. They sure are excited about the baby."

"Yes, they are." Aunt Jean stood by the sink, twisting the hem of her apron. "You know, his father worked for Bill. He and his wife were like family."

"I know. You told me that's why you took Justin in after the accident."

"That was one reason."

Kate added soap and started the dishwasher before facing her sister. "One reason? What other reason was there?"

Aunt Jean cleared her throat nervously. "Let's sit for a minute."

Nova could tell that her aunt was about to have a serious conversation with Grandma Kate. "Do you want me to go upstairs, Aunt Jean?"

"No, honey. I may need protection." She motioned for Nova and Kate to sit at the kitchen table, insisting that Kate take the armchair at the end.

"Jeannie, what's going on? You're making me nervous!"

"I know. I'm sorry. There's just no easy way to tell you this."

"Are you sure I shouldn't leave?" Nova asked, anxious to get out before the bomb went off because that was clearly about to happen. She'd never seen her aunt so worked up.

Aunt Jean shook her head and focused on Kate again. "After you and I had our falling out, I thought about what happened with you and Daniel and the fact that you never found out what happened to him."

"It was just as well..." Kate's eyes filled with tears. "By that time, it was too late."

"Is it ever really too late, sister?"

"What do you mean?" Kate frowned.

"Sometime after our argument, I decided to look for Daniel."

Kate's face turned red. "You what?"

"No point getting angry now. Like I said, it was years ago."

"That was a stupid thing to do! What would have happened if you'd found him? Were you going to just waltz up and say, 'You used to be married to my sister in another life'?"

"Of course not. I didn't say anything like that," Aunt Jean huffed.

Kate's mouth flew open, and all the color drained from her face. "You found him?"

"Yes, I did. He was a widower with a married son."

Kate slumped in her chair and moaned. "How could you do that to me? Didn't you know how much it would hurt?"

"I know it hurts, and I'm sorry to be so blunt. But I need to tell you all of it."

Kate put her face in her hands. "Just stop."

Aunt Jean pulled Kate's hands away. "Listen to me. Bill hired Daniel's son, James, to work for his company. James and his wife, Debra, became like family. They had a beautiful little boy with red hair and blue eyes. He loved the farm, especially the horses. By the time he was a teenager, he was one of the best riders I've ever seen. He was a natural."

Nova felt a chill run up her spine. Her aunt was talking about Justin! Her eyes darted to her grandmother's face. Based on her expression, she had also made the connection.

Aunt Jean continued. "One day, James and his family were in a terrible accident. James and Debra were killed instantly, and their son was badly hurt. He was in the hospital for a long time. When he was well enough, we brought him home."

Kate's voice quivered. "Justin."

Aunt Jean nodded. "I'm telling you now because Justin's grandfather is coming in the morning."

"Daniel? My Daniel?"

"Yes. Your Daniel."

Kate appeared to be near swooning. Nova jumped up, filled a glass with water, and tried to hand it to her grandmother. But Kate stared at the glass as if she had no idea what she should do with it. Nova set it in front of her and returned to her seat.

Aunt Jean took her sister's trembling hand. "This could be a good thing. At the very least, seeing him may bring you some closure."

Kate suddenly came alive, jerking her hand away. "Closure? There won't be any *closure* because I have seen him. Many times! Didn't you hear me before? The three of us were together as a family in the tapestry. I can't bear to see Daniel again as a stranger! And little Danny will still be gone!"

"It's up to you. But I think you'll regret it if you don't." Aunt Jean stood. "Sleep on it. See how you feel in the morning."

"You should have told me before I came all the way down here." Kate pushed her chair back and stormed out of the kitchen and up the stairs.

Aunt Jean stared at the door into the hall as if expecting Kate to come back. Somewhere upstairs, a door slammed.

"She's really mad," Nova said.

Her aunt sat down again. "She'll get over it." She smiled. "Kate's first reaction is always anger, but she usually comes around... eventually."

"If you say so." Nova shook her head. "What's the point anyway? What if we change timelines again and it's all a waste?"

Aunt Jean sighed. "You can't stop living just because you may switch to another timeline. You have to live your life every minute because you don't really know what will happen next."

"Okay. Still... Grandma Kate might not agree with you."

"Let me worry about that, honey." Nova stood, but Aunt Jean motioned for her to sit again. "I have something to tell you too."

"What?" she asked nervously, a lump in her throat.

Aunt Jean laughed. "It's not that bad! I talked to your dad, and he suggested that you and Marshall spend the summer with me at Willow Hill."

Nova's mouth fell open.

Her aunt reached across the table and closed it for her. "You're catching flies again."

Nova wasn't the least bit amused. "How could he just decide that without asking me first? Don't I get any sort of say in this?"

Aunt Jean raised her eyebrows. "Maybe he wanted to surprise you. Besides, we both thought you'd be pleased."

"I'm sorry. But now I won't see Ethan all summer!"

"I thought you wanted to learn about the tapestry." Aunt Jean leaned forward, her arms on the table. "You know, *fix things*?"

"I do! I guess I just thought… I don't know. It didn't occur to me that I wouldn't see Ethan again before I…"

"Before you left this timeline?"

"Yeah, I guess so."

"You came down here planning to travel, didn't you?"

"I did, but…"

"But now you're saying you had planned to go home again first?"

"No… I don't know."

"Nova, you're not making sense."

"I know I'm not. I don't know what's wrong with me." That was the truth. She had every intention of traveling again, of finding a timeline that held both her sister and her little brother. That was the most important thing. So why was she panicked over the idea of spending the summer here? Especially when the summer might not last that long if she changed timelines?

Aunt Jean had been studying Nova while she wrestled with her conflicting emotions. "Why don't we hash this out in the morning? It's been a long day, and we're all tired." She stood and motioned for Nova to do the same. "I'm going to the barn to get Marshall. I can't imagine what he's doing there so late. You run along upstairs, and we'll talk at breakfast."

Nova swung her legs over the bench and headed up to her room. Her reaction to staying at Willow Hill all summer made no sense. Aunt Jean was right. She *had* come planning to travel again. But with her aunt's news, all thoughts of the tapestry and changing timelines had flown out of her head.

All she cared about was seeing Ethan.

Once in bed, Nova stared at the ceiling and tried to make sense of her jumbled thoughts. Maybe Grandma Kate had gotten into her head and stolen her resolve. But what about Alana? She couldn't leave her in oblivion.

Nova squeezed her eyes shut and imagined her sister sitting on the end of the four-poster, begging her not to forget. "You said you were coming back for me…"

"I am," Nova whispered as her determination returned full force. "I promise."

Tomorrow, she would apologize to her aunt and plunge into the process of learning about the tapestry. Tonight, she needed to rest so she'd be clearheaded.

But all the inner turmoil had exhausted her, and it was impossible to relax. The crickets in the garden were unusually loud through the open window, almost as if they were mocking her. She pulled the pillow around her head to blot out the sound. She'd always loved the nighttime melody of the garden… but not tonight. She rose and shut the window for the first time since her arrival at Willow Hill. For a moment, she imagined herself in her bedroom at home with Ethan tapping on her window. The temptation to call him was overwhelming. She shook off the thought, determined not to dwell on anything but restoring her family. Besides, the stress of the evening was catching up to her, and all she wanted to do was sleep.

She closed her eyes, took a deep breath, and slowly let it out, repeating the process over and over. It was no use. Her mind wasn't going to cooperate. Instead, it replayed the entire conversation in the garden with her grandmother and aunt. Frustrated, she got up and opened the window again. A pleasant breeze floated in along with the garden sounds. She lingered there for a few minutes and felt her mind and body relax.

After a while, she climbed into bed again and resumed her rhythmic breathing. Slowly, the crickets faded

away. The only sound she heard now was the clock. Tick...
tock...

"Shut up," she muttered as she drifted off.

CHAPTER 9

Nova rose early the next morning, hoping to see Aunt Jean before anyone else was up and about. Her aunt was bustling around the kitchen as usual. Her cheeks were flushed and her hair, pulled back in the familiar low bun, looked slightly disheveled. It was barely seven o'clock. Nova wondered how long she'd been up.

"Well, look who's awake and ready for the day." Aunt Jean smiled approvingly.

Nova impulsively hugged her aunt. "I wanted to see you, to apologize for being so weird about spending the summer."

Aunt Jean was obviously pleased by the gesture. "No need, honey. I should've asked your opinion on the matter instead of presenting it as a done deal." She turned off the oven and placed a platter of muffins and a bowl of fruit on the table. "This should do for now. I'll make a big lunch. Would you like to help me with something?"

"Uh… sure." Nova looked longingly at the muffins. They smelled delicious.

Aunt Jean smiled. "Why don't you grab a couple of those and follow me?"

Nova didn't need to be told twice. She wrapped two warm muffins in a napkin and followed her aunt up the stairs. "Where are we going?"

"My mother's room. It's down the hall past yours and

mine. I go in there once a week to freshen it up. She likes a clean room."

Nova almost choked on her muffin. "She's not—I mean, she isn't…"

Aunt Jean raised her eyebrows. "In there?"

Nova stopped dead in her tracks. "Oh my God…"

Aunt Jean threw her head back and laughed until tears ran down her face. "Honey, of course she's not there. Oh my, you're the funniest little thing!"

"Not on purpose…" Heat radiated from Nova's cheeks. She didn't think it was all that funny. "The way you talked about her… I just thought…"

"It's all right, honey." Aunt Jean dabbed her eyes, still chuckling. They arrived at the end of the long hallway and a locked door. She studied Nova for a moment, the key in her hand. "You're mighty serious for such a young person."

Nova stared at her feet. "I don't mean to be. I'm sorry."

"No need to be sorry, honey. It's the serious people in this world who usually get things done." She put her arm around Nova. "I know I've probably said this before, but you remind me of my mother. And that's no small thing."

Nova had heard that before but was uncertain as to whether she should be flattered or not. "Is that good? That I'm like her?"

Her aunt looked at her solemnly. "My mother was the strongest person I ever knew. She was the backbone of the family. I can't think of anyone better. So yes, it's a good thing to be like her." She unlocked the door and stepped inside.

Nova's breath caught in her throat. "Aunt Jean, this is amazing."

"It's like she's still here." Aunt Jean smiled.

It was a large room with windows that looked out over the pasture where the mares and foals grazed. A wooden rocking chair with a blue floral cushion was next to a window. An intricately carved canopy bed stood in the center of the room, overlooking the scene. Two high-backed armchairs formed a sitting area, complete with a marble table, antique lamps, and…

Nova gasped. "The clock!"

Aunt Jean gave her a questioning look.

"I hear it all the time and wondered where it was," Nova explained.

"My father bought it as a wedding present for my mother."

"It's beautiful."

"Yes, it is. Mother used to keep it wound, but after she passed away, I left it alone at first. After a while, I started winding it again. I missed it."

Nova tore her eyes away from the grandfather clock and surveyed the rest of the room. The wall opposite the sitting area was occupied by a floor-to-ceiling bookcase that was crammed to capacity with books. An oriental rug graced the dark, mahogany-stained wood floors, giving the expansive room a cozy feel. Various knickknacks littered the room, but instead of making the space seem cluttered, it gave the room a charming ambiance.

Nova's gaze made another sweep, and she noticed a chest very much like the one in her room, except this one was lower and wider and had a swivel mirror on the top. "She must have loved it here."

"She did. This room was her sanctuary."

"It's nice that she lived with you."

"She moved in after my father died."

"The first Dayton Grant," Nova said.

"Yes. And let me tell you, he was so much like your dad. In a lot of ways, he was a big kid, always ready to laugh. Mother used to say he never met a practical joke he didn't like." Aunt Jean shook her head, smiling. "He was the light in our household."

"Like my dad, especially before…"

"Before?"

"Yeah. Before we started traveling. Before I found out about the family *gift*."

Aunt Jean studied her for a moment, then said firmly, "Give him time. He'll be that way again."

"I hope so." Feeling the need to change the subject, she asked, "How long did my great-grandmother live here?"

"She was here for eight years, until she passed away. It's been a long time now, but I can still picture her sitting in that rocking chair, watching the horses. She loved when the foals played in the pasture. Sometimes we'd have two or three at a time, and they'd frolic like little children. She had a hard time getting around toward the end and couldn't go down to the barn very often. Watching the little ones from her room cheered her up and gave her something to look forward to. She knew all their names and who their mammas were. She really kept up with all the horses. She'd always wanted to ride but never had the opportunity. By the time she moved in, she wasn't up to it physically."

"Couldn't she have… never mind."

"I know what you're thinking. Couldn't she have gone back to a time when she'd have been able to?"

"Yeah."

Aunt Jean sat in her mother's rocker and gazed out the window. Nova could picture her years from now, watching the horses out the window as Evelyn had done.

"She was happy with her life, I guess. She didn't want to risk changing anything."

Nova nodded. "If Alana and Marshall were both here, I'd never travel again either. I wouldn't want to take a chance of losing them."

Aunt Jean stared out the window at the horses grazing in the pasture. A colt trotted up and down the fence line, and every so often, he leapt into the air and kicked his heels, as if showing off for the others.

"That one's going to be a handful." She turned her attention back to Nova. "As for not traveling again, see how you feel down the road. You never know. My mother did a lot of traveling for much of her life. Once she stopped though, that was it."

"Why do you keep her room locked?"

Aunt Jean chuckled. "You'll understand when you meet Miles, Henry, Lily, and Maisy—Michael's kids. Let's just say that they can be quite *precocious*. It means a lot to me to keep this room as it is."

"I can understand that. When my dad was killed in the wreck, I didn't want anything to change in his office. Mom knew what it meant to me to have it just like he'd left it, so she kept it the same. I don't think she could've gone in there anyway. She sort of fell apart after he was gone. We all did."

"That must have been hard. I bet you still struggle with his death even though you have him back."

She was right. Deep down, Nova still worried that death would somehow reach out its icy fingers and snatch him away. She'd never gotten over losing him. It had stained her world in a way that could never be fully washed away.

"All of us died a little with him. We never laughed anymore." Nova teared up just thinking about her other life. "My mom was the worst. She was like a different person." The image of her mother sitting at the kitchen table and circling want ads while the sun glinted off her orange hair popped into her brain. Nova sighed. "My dad was so much fun. She always accused him of being a big kid. I always thought it was something that bothered her, but after he was gone..."

"Your mother missed it," Aunt Jean finished for her.

"We all did." It was surprising how deeply she could still feel his loss even though he was alive and well.

"It was the same with my father." Aunt Jean sighed, then stood and raised the window. "We best get started."

She pulled a feather duster from a shelf in the closet and began running it over the furniture.

Feeling as though she should be helping instead of watching her aunt work, Nova asked, "What should I do?"

"I thought you might want to look around. This will only take a few minutes."

Something dawned on Nova. "Is this where Evelyn kept her journal?"

Aunt Jean stopped dusting and looked at her. "I always thought so, but for some reason, it disappeared after Mother died."

"You must have found it. You gave it to me. Or rather, you left it for me in the chest in my room here."

"I did?"

"Yes. It was in the timeline with Alana." Nova decided to leave out the part about her aunt being dead at the time.

Aunt Jean frowned. "It must be here somewhere then, but I've looked... many times."

"I found it taped to the bottom of a drawer. The only way to see it was to take the drawer out."

Her aunt walked over to the chest and pulled out the drawers, one after the other. Sure enough, the journal was taped carefully to the bottom of a lower drawer. "Well, what do you know?" She cradled the journal lovingly. "Why on earth did she go to such lengths to hide it?"

"Maybe because she didn't want you to read about the tapestry. She thought it was dangerous."

"Maybe..." Aunt Jean looked at the book for a long moment, then handed it to Nova. "I obviously wanted you to have this."

***

Nova spent the rest of the day reading the journal again, only pausing long enough to eat lunch and dinner with the family. Marshall was disappointed that she wouldn't come to the barn again, but Nova was determined to absorb as much knowledge as she possibly could from her great-grandmother's words. By evening, it was all she could do to hold her eyes open. She finally put down the book a little after ten.

She soaked in the claw-foot tub and tried to make sense of the cryptic passages until her head ached. It was time to rest. Besides, the water was becoming unpleasantly cool.

She fell asleep almost the instant her head hit the pillow.

Someone was tapping lightly on the window. Nova raised her head and looked around. The light from the street lamp outside allowed her to see just enough to realize she was back at home. She could almost make out the Time Machine *poster with the missing tack on her wall. She turned her attention to the window as the tapping grew louder. She could just make out a silhouette against the glow of the street lamp.*

Ethan! She jumped out of bed but stopped halfway to the window.

"Nova, let me in!" It wasn't Ethan's voice. It was Alana's. "You said you'd come back for me..."

CHAPTER 10

A clap of thunder woke Nova early. She struggled to shake off the dream, her heart still pounding. It took a few minutes for her jumbled thoughts to fall into place as she surveyed her surroundings. Her room had a twilight quality, hovering between light and dark. She figured that it could be later in the morning than it seemed because of the cloud cover blotting out the sun.

She lay in bed, listening to the storm. All was peaceful for a moment, then came the crack of lightning followed by rumbling thunder. It seemed symbolic, the weather acting out her life. She let her mind wander back to her home in Connecticut and the dream that had seemed so real. It was easy to imagine Alana running into her room any moment. "Wow! Did you hear that one? It was close!" Her fearless sister loved thunderstorms. It never occurred to her to be afraid. Nova wished for the thousandth time that she were more like her.

She missed Alana desperately, and the dream had amplified those feelings. Why were they wasting so much time? They needed to figure out how to use the tapestry to get her back. That was all that mattered now. She had to put aside her feelings for Ethan. He had been in every timeline so far, and he would be in the next one. She wasn't going to lose him—she felt sure of that. When she found the right reality, she'd meet him as she had before and never have to start over again.

Someone knocked on her door softly. "Nova, are you planning to sleep all day?" It was Aunt Jean.

"I'm awake," Nova answered. "I'm just listening to the storm."

Aunt Jean opened her door. She was carrying a stack of linens. "I have a few things to do this morning. Want to help?"

"Sure. Then can we talk?"

"Maybe later today." Aunt Jean smiled. "It may get kind of busy around here."

Nova's heart fell. She'd almost forgotten about Michael's family coming to visit.

Her aunt noticed her crestfallen expression. "Don't worry, honey. It'll all work out."

"But I don't want to wait. What's the point?"

"Don't dismiss today because of what you want for tomorrow."

"That sounds like a fortune cookie."

Her aunt laughed. "I guess it does. Still good advice though. And don't you think we need to wait for your dad? Your parents will be back here to celebrate your birthday, you know."

"Maybe Dad doesn't care if we travel without him. If he cared, he wouldn't have let me stay for the summer without him."

"Oh, I think he has a plan to keep you in this timeline."

"What do you mean?" Nova asked. "How will he do that?"

"Just wait and see…"

"I hate it when you do that."

Nova could hear her aunt laughing all the way down the hall. She jumped out of bed and peered into the hallway just in time to see her aunt enter one of the guest rooms on the other side of the stairs.

Nova took her time bathing and dressing. When she stepped into the kitchen sometime later, Aunt Jean and Grandma Kate were laughing like a couple of schoolgirls.

"There you are!" Kate was positively glowing in white jeans and a powder-blue blouse that brought out her blue eyes. Her hair was pulled back in a flattering style that made her look years younger.

For a split second, Nova wondered if she'd traveled back in time.

Aunt Jean chuckled. "Kate saw Daniel this morning."

"Oh, Grandma, I'm so glad!" Nova beamed. This Grandma Kate was a far cry from the one they'd left in Frederick. Nova could see why Daniel had been smitten with her so many years ago.

"I've decided to 'go for it,' as you teenagers like to say."

"I think everyone says that. Everyone except you, that is." Aunt Jean laughed.

"Fine. Laugh all you want. Nothing can dampen my mood. But don't spring anything else on me this trip, or I'll end up in a jar on your mantel, just like Matthew."

Nova gasped and looked at Aunt Jean. "Uncle Matthew is in a jar?"

"He said he didn't want to be in the ground. He wanted to be where I had to look at him every day." Aunt Jean grinned. "So now he is. Besides, this way I can talk to him anytime I want to."

"Let me know if he talks back." Kate shook her head but laughed all the same. "I think cremation is morbid."

"Ashes to ashes, sister."

Kate ignored her and turned to Nova. "Daniel is just as I remember him. So handsome!"

"So, how did it go—seeing him again?" Nova asked enthusiastically. She loved seeing this side of her grandmother.

Aunt Jean jumped in. "I was almost singed from all

the sparks flying around the room!"

"Very funny." Kate blushed.

"Muffins are still on the table, Nova." Aunt Jean smiled. "Help yourself. We'll have lunch the usual time."

"Okay. Maybe I'll go down to the barn for a while. Or the garden…" Nova was anxious to be alone with her thoughts.

"The garden is nice this time of morning, especially after a good rain. If you go to the barn, you're liable to be put to work."

"Good point." Nova agreed, grabbing a blueberry muffin.

"Kate and I have a few things to do. You run along." She winked at Kate.

What's she up to? Nova wondered as she shuffled down the path to the gazebo.

Aunt Jean was right. The garden seemed especially beautiful this morning, as if there had been an explosion of color. Raindrops clung to the delicate petals like tiny prisms reflecting the sunlight. The effect was stunning.

She climbed the steps into the gazebo and sat in a wicker chair with her feet up on the matching ottoman. A robin perched on one of the hanging flower baskets, watching her. Aunt Jean often fed the birds, so they had lost most of their fear of humans.

"Hey, little guy," Nova said softly.

The robin cocked his head to the side and listened. She pinched off a piece of muffin and laid it on the rail. He hopped down from his perch to retrieve it.

Nova glanced around the gazebo and felt like crying. In spite of the beauty surrounding her, she couldn't shake off her sense of melancholy. She imagined Alana sitting opposite her in one of the other wicker chairs. If she could have changed places with her, she would have.

"I hope I'm up to this," Nova whispered.

Her imaginary sister's mouth was curved up in that

familiar smile. "Come back to the tapestry, little sister…"

"I'm working on it," Nova whispered.

The robin flew off as if not wanting to intrude. Nova leaned her head back and closed her eyes, but her mind was in overdrive, thinking of Alana and traveling. Something bothered her. Aunt Jean had said that there was only one of each of them. But then why was Nova able to see herself in countless lives when she was in the tapestry? Weren't those other Novas living as well? Even more disturbing, was another Nova looking into this timeline right now? A chill ran up her spine. Maybe the other versions of herself were ghostly impressions as fleeting as the timelines they occupied. She hoped Aunt Jean was right—that there weren't other Novas. Her aunt seemed to know all about traveling. But she hadn't known about the tapestry. She'd thought it wasn't real. So, if she had been wrong about that, maybe she was wrong about this too.

Nova heard Justin's truck pull up to the house and wondered what he'd been up to so early. There was so much to do at the barn in the morning: feeding and watering the horses, turning them out in the pastures, and mucking out the stalls. Maybe he'd gone into town to buy more feed… or maybe he'd gone to pick up Michael, Julia, and the kids. Nova decided to hang out in the garden and avoid the chaos as long as possible.

It wasn't long before she heard someone coming down the path to the gazebo. She wasn't in the mood to talk to anyone and considered making a run for it.

Too late. As he stepped into view, Nova gasped and flung herself at him, knocking the air out of his lungs before he had a chance to speak.

After a brief fit of coughing, he managed, "What's up, hot girl?"

CHAPTER 11

"Ethan!" Nova kissed him tenderly. "I can't believe it!"

He cupped her chin. "I guess you're glad to see me, huh?"

"Oh my God, you have no idea! But how did you get here?"

"Your dad called my parents and asked if I could come. They were surprisingly okay with the idea. Your parents bought me a plane ticket, and Justin picked me up at the airport." He wrapped his arms around her. "So... you're okay that I'm here for the rest of the summer? You're not mad?"

"Of course I'm not mad! Why would I be?"

"The last time we hung out, I told you to leave. I'm sorry about that, by the way."

Nova was confused. "When was that?"

"At my house... on my birthday."

"Oh..." Nova tried to focus on this timeline. It was becoming more and more difficult to separate the memories from each one. "You came to my window the night before I left, right?"

"Yeah." Ethan frowned. "It's only been a few days. Do you even remember what I said to you?"

"I remember. But a lot's happened since then."

Ethan stepped back. "What do you mean? You don't

feel the same?"

Nova threw her arms around him again. "Of course I do. That won't ever change." She laid her head on his chest and felt his heart pounding.

He stroked her hair. "I'm sorry. I know you've been through a lot... traveling, I mean. But you're still here. That's all I care about."

"So you were the company that was coming," she said softly.

"What?"

Nova chuckled. "I thought Michael and his family were coming. I've been dreading it. But all the time it was you. My dad's pretty smart."

"Okay..."

Nova laughed. "I'll explain later. I'm just glad you're not a bunch of cousins." She grabbed his hand and pulled him up the path to the house.

"Where are we going?"

"My room."

"Works for me." He grinned.

"Get over yourself!" She giggled. "I want you to see the attic."

"Your room is in the attic?"

"Of course not. But the access is in my room."

They burst through the door from the veranda to a surprised Aunt Jean and Grandma Kate.

"Where are you two headed in such a hurry? I thought you'd take Ethan down to the barn to see the horses."

"I'll do that later, Aunt Jean," Nova answered as she flew through the kitchen with Ethan in tow. "I want to show him the house."

Nova practically dragged him up the stairs.

"I can walk on my own, you know," he said.

She gripped his hand even tighter and laughed. "Come on."

When she flung open the door to her room, Ethan

jumped in ahead of her and pulled her into a passionate kiss.

"I've been wanting to do that since you left." He kissed her again, and she came away breathless.

"That's not why we're up here, you know." Nova playfully poked him in the ribs.

"Okay, hot girl." He gave her a smug grin. "Where's this attic?"

"Over here." Nova opened the door next to her bed.

Ethan stuck his head in the dark space and groaned. "Seriously? You've actually been up there?"

"It's not as bad as it looks." She pulled the chain, and the bulb clicked on, revealing the rough wood stairs.

"Oh yeah. That's much better."

"Don't be a smartass." She trotted up the stairs and pulled the other chain at the top, then looked back at him. "Coming?"

"I'm thinking."

"Ethan, get up here." She giggled.

He cautiously followed her up the stairs and paused at the door to the attic. "Are you sure it's okay to come up here?"

"Oh my God. Can you be a bigger chicken?"

"Maybe I should have mentioned before that I don't like small, dark spaces…"

"It's not that small, and it's not that dark. Man up."

"This is an interesting side of you, by the way," he said as he shuffled along the wall.

Nova chuckled. "You said that before."

"I did? When?"

"When we drove to Frederick," Nova blurted before remembering that he didn't know about going to Frederick in the previous timeline. This Ethan had never been to her grandmother's house. That was the other one, the one who was probably still sitting on the bed, holding her hand in Connecticut. She shook herself mentally. *For the last time, there aren't other Ethans, you idiot!*

"Um… what are you talking about?"

"Sorry. That was… it doesn't matter." Nova felt her cheeks go red.

Ethan frowned. "Are you okay?"

"Yeah. Just confused for a minute. I'm mixing up my timelines, I guess."

"So, of course you and I did things in this other timeline… like going to a place called Frederick," he mused.

"It's where my grandmother lived… or lives."

"You took me to see your grandmother?" He stood next to her and gave her a half smile. "What for?"

"To talk to her about Marshall."

His intense blue eyes stared into hers. "What else did we do in that timeline? You and me?"

Nova's heart quickened, and she had the overwhelming urge to throw her arms around him and kiss him, like she'd done in the parking lot after her disastrous birthday party. But what would be the point? She was leaving this timeline too. "It doesn't matter. I'm back here now."

He didn't seem to know what else to say, so after an awkward moment, he moved around the room.

"What are you doing?"

He'd made a sweep of the entire area and was back at the door. "I'm getting my bearings."

Nova gave him a mischievous smile. "Look up."

He did, and a doll stared down at him with her lifeless eyes. "Jeez! What the heck is that?"

"A little shrunken person." Nova giggled.

"Not funny." He made his way to the center of the room, where she was kneeling by a trunk. "Don't do that!"

"You think that's bad…" She flung open the trunk full of dolls.

Ethan fell backward, kicking up a fine cloud of dust. "Holy crap!" He clutched his chest as if he were having a heart attack. "Are you trying to kill me?"

He grabbed her and pulled her down with him. Nova

managed to wriggle away and fell into a fit of laughter.

"Okay, sorry. Don't feel too bad. I almost passed out the first time I saw them. There's a much better trunk over here." Nova took his hand and pulled him over to the massive trunk in the center of the room. "No more dolls. I swear." She raised the lid and carefully pulled out the painting on top. "This is my grandmother's first family."

Ethan moved in closer and studied it. "She was divorced?"

"No. It's her first family from another timeline."

"Really? That's a painting of people from another timeline?" He was clearly struggling to wrap his head around the concept that there could actually be evidence that someone had had other lives. "They have pictures of these people… are they hanging all over the house?"

Nova rolled her eyes. "Of course not. That would be creepy."

"Thank you. I was searching for the right word, but *creepy* works."

"Something really tragic happened to Grandma Kate's first family, and I guess my aunt thought she'd want to remember them someday. So, she painted this picture. See?" Nova pointed out the signature. "J. G. Huckaby is Jean Grant Huckaby. My aunt Jean."

"What happened to them?"

"Her husband, Daniel, was killed when their little boy was a couple of years old. Grandma Kate tried to go back in time to fix it, but it didn't work. She lost them both."

"So the husband and child in this picture are dead?"

"The little boy was never born." She almost added, "Like Marshall." But Marshall was back, and Alana was dead again. Remorse threatened to overtake her, but she forced it down somewhere deep inside. *I'll find a way if it kills me…*

"What about her husband?"

"Daniel had another family. He never met my

grandmother, as far as he knew. Well, not until now. Aunt Jean and Uncle Bill hired his son years ago. Justin is his grandson. He's here visiting."

"So, he has no idea that she already knows him? That there's a picture of him in the attic?"

"Right."

"Wow." He shook his head. "It sucks about the kid though. How would you get over something like that?"

"You don't. It made my grandmother really bitter. I remember that she never seemed happy when I was little." Nova studied the picture for a moment before laying it on the floor. "Let's talk about something else."

"Sure. What's in the bags?" Ethan reached into the trunk and hauled out a cloth bag. "This is heavy." He dumped the contents on the floor and whistled.

"They're pirate coins." Nova picked one up and handed it to him.

"Okay, this is cool. How did the old girl get these? Were some of your ancestors pirates?"

"Honestly, I have no idea. I never asked her."

"You're kidding."

"No. I guess it never came up."

"Are you kids up there?" Aunt Jean called from the bottom of the stairs.

Ethan nearly jumped out of his skin. "Do you think she heard me?"

"The *old girl* just put out a platter of sandwiches for lunch," Aunt Jean said.

Nova looked at Ethan. "I'd say that's a yes."

CHAPTER 12

"We'll be right down," Nova called.

Ethan grimaced. "Should I stay up here?"

"My aunt has a great sense of humor. She probably won't poison you or anything." Nova giggled.

"Great." He reluctantly followed her down the stairs to the kitchen.

Sure enough, a platter of sandwiches was on the kitchen table. Aunt Jean stuck a tray of cookies in the oven before turning around.

"I'm sorry about the *old girl* remark, Mrs. ... uh..."

Aunt Jean threw her head back and laughed. "You don't know how true that is."

"Oh, right. Because of the time travel thing, I guess. You don't look that old though. I mean, for someone who..." Ethan looked to Nova for help getting out of this awkward situation, but she grinned and shook her head.

Aunt Jean raised her eyebrows, clearly amused. "Someone who...?"

He looked down and shuffled his feet.

"Nobody calls me Mrs. Huckaby. Call me Aunt Jean." She grabbed a couple of plates from the pantry and handed one to each of them. "Have a sandwich. We keep a pretty tight schedule around here as far as meals go, even if you sleep all morning." She winked at Nova before turning to Ethan. "You may have to wait until you swallow that foot in your mouth though."

"Yes, ma'am," Ethan answered sheepishly.

Watching him squirm was fun, but Nova decided to help him out by changing the subject. "Aren't the others coming in for lunch?"

"I sent sandwiches down there earlier. Marshall wanted to eat at the barn. That boy would sleep down there if we let him."

"Where's Grandma Kate?"

"She's gone to town with Daniel. I swear it's just like before. Smitten. Both of them."

"That's pretty fast," Nova said between bites.

"That's how it happened years ago. That's why our parents were so against it. But they came around eventually."

"Because of the little boy."

Nova regretted mentioning him when her aunt dabbed her eyes on her apron. "Yes. Because of Danny." Aunt Jean sat across from them at the table and motioned toward Ethan. "How much did you tell him?"

"Not all of it, but enough."

"I wouldn't say anything, Mrs.—Aunt Jean," he stammered.

"I know you won't. Now eat up. The cookies will be out soon."

Nova and Ethan complied by scarfing down two sandwiches each, which seemed to please her greatly. Other than the sound of chewing, the kitchen was quiet.

Nova figured that Ethan was trying to avoid sticking his foot in his mouth again. She looked at him and stuck out her tongue.

"Stop it," he mouthed.

When the timer on the oven chimed, Aunt Jean took out the cookies and placed them on a cooling rack.

After they'd cooled a bit, she loaded them onto a plate. "Why don't you kids take these to the barn? I bet Marshall could eat at least a half dozen."

Ethan shot out of his chair like a rocket, and Nova had to stifle a laugh.

She laughed when they were halfway down the hill. "What's wrong with you?"

"I have no idea. Maybe you should back us up to this morning and let me start over."

"Nice try, but it's not that easy."

"Fine. Just don't be surprised if you get 'the talk' from your aunt later."

"What talk?"

"The 'Why on earth are you with that loser?' talk."

"Oh, get over yourself. It hasn't been that bad. Okay… well, maybe it has." She playfully jabbed him in the side. "You just need to be yourself."

Aunt Jean hollered out the back door, "Make sure Connie and Justin get some of those cookies!"

"We will!" Nova called back.

Marshall came running out of the barn, dragging the water hose. He obviously didn't have the valve closed all the way, because he was leaving a soggy trail. "What's on the plate?"

"You don't have to be so loud." Nova held out the plate. "They're cookies. And you're making a mess!"

Marshall twisted the dial at the end of the hose, shutting it off most of the way. A small stream of water trickled out and down his leg, soaking his boot. "Dang!" he huffed.

"You're still leaking," Nova pointed out.

"I know!" He twisted the valve again, which seemed to work this time. "Sorry. I don't usually do that. Don't tell Justin, okay?"

"I don't think you'll have to." Nova pointed at the tiny river he'd left behind.

"Oh man!" He looked at Ethan, embarrassed.

"It's okay, Marshall." Ethan smiled. "You should see the messes I make at my parents' nursery."

"And you should see his room," Nova added.

Ethan goosed her in the side, and she jerked away, laughing.

"Cut it out, you guys. You're gonna drop the cookies!" Marshall said.

"Here you go, kiddo. But they're for everyone. Not just you, okay?"

"Sure!" Marshall grabbed them and took off.

Nova turned to Ethan. "We don't have to stay at the barn if you'd rather do something else."

"No, this is great. I love horses. You think we could go riding?"

"You know how?"

"Yeah. I used to ride every summer at camp."

Nova was impressed. "I can't believe you know how to ride. I've only been on a horse once. And that was yesterday."

Justin rode across the field on Sonny. When he reached the barn, he pulled up in front of them. "What are you two up to?"

He winked at Nova, and she felt the usual rush of blood to her cheeks. He apparently knew all about Ethan.

"Do you think we could go riding? Ethan knows how."

Justin smiled. "That's what I hear." He rubbed Sonny's neck. "I guess Ethan could take Doc out today. He's a little more horse than Bo and Marilyn, but I think Ethan can handle him. Doc used to steeplechase like Sonny. We retired him about four years ago. He loves to take it easy on the trails now."

Nova wasn't sure. "He's more horse? What exactly does that mean?"

Ethan spoke up. "It's okay. It just means he's a little harder to handle."

"He's hard to handle?" She wasn't at all sure that Doc was a good idea.

Justin shook his head. "Not so much that. It's just that he's up for anything, like galloping in the field or jumping. Don't worry, Nova. He's a good horse. I'm sure he'll be fine on a slow ride."

"It'll be okay," Ethan assured her. "I promise."

Justin hopped off of Sonny and draped the reins over his shoulder. "I need to get this guy cleaned up, but I'll get Luke to tack up Marilyn and Doc."

"Who's Luke?" Nova asked.

"He's a college kid who comes out here a few days a week to help during the summer. I give him riding lessons as a trade-off. He's getting pretty good. I might even take him to the Saratoga Springs Steeplechase with me in August."

"I don't remember him being here before," Nova blurted out before she could stop herself. Then it dawned on her—the first time she was in this timeline, she'd left before now. So in all likelihood, she would have met Luke if she'd waited to travel.

Justin continued, seemingly unaware of her blunder. "This is his third summer coming around. Of course, he's only here a couple of weekends a month when he's in school. He goes to NC State in Raleigh. He's studying to be a vet."

A lanky young man with dark-brown hair came walking toward them from the barn.

"Luke, this is Jean's great-niece, Nova, and her boyfriend, Ethan."

"Great to meet both of you." He smiled and shook hands.

"I told them you'd tack up Marilyn and Doc. They're going trail riding."

"Sure, Justin." He took off back to the barn.

Less than ten minutes later, Luke reappeared, leading the two horses.

Nova was a little nervous about going out on their own. "Are you sure this is okay?" She directed her question to Justin.

"You'll be fine," Justin reassured her. "Marilyn will take care of you. She's pretty much on autopilot when there are other horses to follow. Why don't you two check out the old caretaker's house? It's about a hundred years old. I go out there once in a while to check on things. Connie and I used to picnic under the big oak tree in the front yard, but we haven't since she got pregnant. Anyway, it's a peaceful spot."

"That sounds fun, I guess," Nova said.

"Just take the trail across the field beyond the riding ring. You'll see the entrance. It's pretty well-worn."

"Isn't that the one we took before?" Nova asked.

"Sure is." Justin adjusted the stirrups on Doc's saddle, then handed the reins to Ethan. "When you get to the clearing, take the trail to the left instead of the one straight ahead."

Nova mounted reluctantly but quickly forgot her reservations when it became obvious that the horses were perfectly happy to stroll along the trail without any effort from their riders. As they made their way through the woods, Nova marveled at Ethan's ease on horseback. It was one more thing about him that she'd probably have known if she could remember anything that had happened in this timeline before the morning she'd passed out in the driveway. From his perspective, very little time had passed since that day. But from hers, it seemed like an eternity ago.

The trail narrowed, and he rode ahead of her on Doc. Marilyn fell in behind the other horse and plodded through the puddles left by the earlier downpour without hesitation. It was as if she barely noticed. Several large roots protruded up from the mud, and she stepped over them without stumbling. Nova relaxed and patted her on the neck.

Ethan looked back. "Where's the clearing Justin was talking about?"

Nova strained to see ahead. "It should be soon. I've only been here once, you know."

The trail widened again, and Ethan let her catch up

until the two horses were side by side. They walked for a few minutes, then Ethan urged Doc forward until he broke into a trot, followed by a willing Marilyn. Nova bounced up and down in the saddle.

"This is too fast," she managed to get out.

"It's not hard. Just pay attention to the one-two beat when her feet hit the ground. Push up on one and sit down in the saddle on two."

Nova watched Ethan as he effortlessly rose and fell with the rhythm of his horse's gait. She concentrated on the beat, attempting to go up and down as Marilyn trotted along the trail. After a few minutes, she had it.

"Hey! This isn't so hard!"

Ethan laughed. "You're a natural."

Now that they were moving at a good clip, it wasn't long before they found themselves in the clearing of flowers.

Ethan whistled. "Who planted all these?"

"I don't know." Nova hadn't thought to ask Justin when they were there before. "They're wildflowers. They probably grew on their own."

"I don't think so. It would be really unusual for this many flowers to grow in one spot without help. Maybe your aunt planted some and they multiplied."

"That's right. I forgot you were a flower boy." Nova giggled.

He rolled his eyes. "Thanks."

"Maybe I'll start calling you that," she offered sweetly.

"Not if you want me to answer you." He laughed. "This is where we turn left."

Ethan's horse turned as quickly as the words were out of his mouth, and Marilyn followed dutifully.

Nova almost fell off. "Oh my God! Slow down!"

Ethan looked back. "Oh, sorry!" He pulled back on the reins, and his horse stopped immediately. Marilyn stopped too. "I'm really sorry. Are you okay?"

Nova tried to catch her breath. "Yeah. Let's just walk now."

"Sure." Doc pawed the ground but stood obediently while Nova recovered.

Ethan backed Doc up until, once again, the horses were side by side. "Are you ready to keep going?" He patted Marilyn on the neck. "She's a good horse."

"I wish I could take her home with me," Nova said. In spite of nearly falling off, Nova enjoyed riding the gentle mare. She could see why Connie loved her so much.

They entered another section of woods but came quickly to an open area much larger than the first clearing. Across the field, tucked into a grove of trees, was a modest farmhouse with a porch that wrapped around the side. The paint had peeled off in areas, and the front porch seemed to sag on one side. A stone walk, bordered on one side by a wooden rail, led to the steps.

"I'm guessing that's where we tie up the horses," Ethan commented.

"Tie them up?" Nova was horrified.

"Not literally, hot girl. Just loop Marilyn's reins over the rail a couple of times so she doesn't wander off."

"Are we going inside? I'm not sure we should."

"Why not? Justin made it sound like no one lives here."

"That's right. But it still seems wrong to snoop around."

"Let's at least take a look." Ethan swung his leg over the saddle and dropped easily to the ground.

He led Doc to the rail and looped the reins over it two times. Doc stood patiently while Ethan helped Nova down and secured Marilyn next to him.

The front door was locked, but a window around the side was cracked open. Ethan managed to slip his hand underneath and raise it up.

"You're not crawling in the window, are you?"

Ethan grinned. "I do it all the time at your house."

Nova blushed. "That's not the same thing."

He shimmied inside and stuck out his hand. "Are you coming?"

CHAPTER 13

Nova reluctantly climbed in after him. The house had a musty smell that reminded her of the trunk in the attic at home. They were standing in a front room devoid of any furniture. It looked as if it had hardly been used. Even though the wide plank floorboards seemed old, they still had some of their original sheen. By contrast, the floorboards in the entry hall were dull and worn.

"I wonder what this room was for. It doesn't look like he used it that much," Nova said quietly. "Look at the floor."

"Why are you whispering?" Ethan asked, clearly amused. "Are you thinking about ghosts?"

"Of course not," she answered at a normal volume. "I'm just uncomfortable."

"You know, it would make perfect sense for the house to be haunted. An old man, living alone, dies under suspicious circumstances…"

Nova rolled her eyes. "Very funny. He didn't die under suspicious circumstances."

Ethan rubbed his chin. "How do you know?"

"I just know. Someone would have said something about it." She pushed past him. "Let's get this over with."

He followed her through the front hall and into the dining room. An old table with a crack down the middle took up the center of the room, but there were no chairs.

"Maybe the place was looted," Ethan offered.

"I doubt it. I think he was here a long time before Aunt Jean and Uncle Bill bought it. When he died, they probably just gave some of the furniture away."

They continued through the downstairs. A small room in the back contained an old rolltop desk and a wooden desk chair on wheels. Ethan opened the drawer in the desk. It was filled with old pictures, mostly of the property. They fanned though them, but Nova couldn't tell where they had been taken. Her relatives had obviously made so many changes that much of the property was unrecognizable.

"Willow Hill is so beautiful, but it seems kind of sad that it's changed so much. He probably loved the land just as it was."

"Where did he go when they bought it?" Ethan asked.

"Nowhere. He stayed here as the caretaker. They offered to build him a new house, but he didn't want it."

"Sounds like a pretty cool old guy."

"Yeah, I guess he was," Nova said. "He probably made a lot of money selling this place, but it didn't change him. This was still his home."

A surprisingly roomy kitchen was next to the office. Someone had left a vase of flowers by the sink. It looked as though it could have been there for years, as the flowers in it had nearly disintegrated.

"That's sad, don't you think?" Nova said solemnly.

"It's pretty bleak. Did he have a family?" Ethan asked.

"I don't know. I can't imagine living here like this. The house wouldn't be so bad if it were fixed up. But it's depressing like it is."

"It's a cool house though. The ceiling must be twelve feet high, and my mom would go crazy for the heavy molding."

"Molding? Are you thinking of being a builder, or maybe a decorator?" Nova gave him a wry smile.

"You've seen my room. What do you think?"

Nova laughed. "I think no one would hire you—not as a decorator anyway."

"Funny. Seriously though. I wonder what they're planning to do with this place. Maybe you and I could fix it up some day. You know, when we're older and married." He winked.

"Are you proposing?" She clutched her chest and feigned excitement.

"Not if you're gonna be that way about it." He laughed. "Besides, I have a plan."

"What plan?"

"You'll have to wait and see."

Nova jabbed him in the side and took off upstairs. At the top of the stairs was a window that overlooked the backyard. Ethan flipped the lock and raised the window enough to stick his head out. Across the property and off to the right was an iron gate that led into an area encircled by a three-foot stone wall. Inside the enclosure, what looked like headstones protruded above the wall.

"Is that a graveyard?" he asked excitedly.

Nova leaned out and looked. "Yeah. Aunt Jean said there was one on the property."

"Cool! Do you know who's buried there?"

"Uncle Bill and Aunt Georgia. Justin's parents too, I think."

"I wonder what happened to the caretaker."

"Oh, he's there too."

"That's awesome! We have to go down there."

Ethan sounded way too enthusiastic as far as Nova was concerned. She wasn't anxious to visit her dead relatives buried behind a secluded old house that, for all intents and purposes, could be haunted by those very relatives.

"You're not afraid, are you?" He actually looked hopeful.

Nova had the urge to elbow him in the side again. "Sorry to disappoint you, but no," she lied.

There was no way she would give him the satisfaction of knowing how uncomfortable she was. Up until now, she would have said that she didn't believe in ghosts. But apparently the five-year-old Nova who thought monsters were under her bed had returned and taken over the logic section of her brain.

Ethan grabbed her hand, practically dragging her down the stairs. "Come on, hot girl. I'll protect you."

"You don't want to look around the rest of the upstairs?" she said breathlessly.

"Nah. This is better."

"But there are at least three other rooms…"

Ethan pulled her through the kitchen, out the back door. The cemetery was about five hundred feet from the house. Ethan yanked on the iron gate at the entrance, but it wouldn't budge.

"Try pushing instead of pulling," Nova suggested.

He pushed, and the gate creaked open. "I don't think anyone's been here in a while."

Nova agreed. Dead branches were littered about, probably blown in during storms, and the lot was overgrown with weeds. The cemetery was larger than it had looked from the upstairs window. Part of the land extended into the woods behind it. In the center was a monument engraved with the Grant name in old English letters, and granite benches sat in each corner. Directly in front of the monument were two neatly maintained graves. One read "Georgia Bernard Grant," and the other read "William Harris Grant." About twenty feet behind the monument was another grave. The stone read "Patrick Willis O'Malley."

"I think that's him," Nova said quietly. "The caretaker." To the right of the monument were two other headstones. "Those are Justin's parents. His dad worked for Uncle Bill."

"Was your aunt married?"

"Yeah. His name was Matthew Huckaby. He died

too."

"Where is he?" Ethan asked.

"Burned up."

Ethan's mouth fell open. "What?"

She laughed. "Bad joke, sorry. He's in a jar on the mantel. Aunt Jean had him cremated. Apparently, he didn't want to be in the ground."

"Oh." He chuckled. "You're sick, by the way."

"Yeah, well…"

"What's that one over there?" Ethan pointed at a grave on the far side. The headstone was different than the others. It was in the shape of a flattened-out barrel. Engraved across the middle were the words "Cisco. Loyal friend."

"That's Uncle Bill's horse."

"They buried a horse in the family cemetery?"

"Yeah. He was the only horse my great-uncle rode. He really loved him. Connie said after Uncle Bill died, Cisco would still come to the fence looking for him."

"That's pretty cool." Ethan ran his hand over the letters. "Your family is a little weird… but amazing. I'd give anything to have a place like this."

Nova took his hand. "Maybe you will someday."

Ethan turned to her, an odd expression on his face. "Nova…"

Her heart jumped into her throat. He rarely called her Nova. She laid her head against his chest and closed her eyes. "What's wrong?"

He sat on one of the benches, and she settled in beside him. Birds chattered in the cluster of trees next to the cemetery. It was a sound Nova had grown to love. She laid her head on his shoulder.

"I was just thinking. I know you plan to travel again, and I understand why you want to. But every time you do, we lose memories. I don't want to forget being here with you. And I might never be here again."

"I hate the thought of losing times like this too." She

didn't know what else to say. Even if she did, it wouldn't change anything. She didn't have a choice. She had to save her family, and losing Ethan over and over was the price of traveling. "I have to go back for Alana. I miss her so much."

"I know you do." His tone was one of resignation. "So, what's the plan?"

Nova hadn't told him on the phone about the tapestry. She'd just said that she had managed to find the timeline back. Now she didn't have the energy to go into it. Better to leave that part out anyway. He already knew more than he should. She looked up and met his intense blue eyes. He was waiting for a response.

"I have an idea, but I need to work it out. I'll tell you all about it later. I promise." That could very well turn out to be another lie, but telling him the truth would be worse. "Right now, I just want to be with you."

That much was true. At the moment, all she wanted was to stay in his arms and forget about everything else.

"Whatever you say, hot girl."

CHAPTER 14

"Hey, you two."

Nova nearly jumped out of her skin.

It was Justin. Neither of them had noticed him ride up on Sonny. "It's about time to get the horses back to the barn. We'll be feeding them soon."

"Sorry." Nova's cheeks were warm. At least Ethan looked embarrassed too. "I guess we lost track of time."

"No problem. I'll wait in front with the horses." Justin turned Sonny and disappeared around the side of the house.

"I bet Aunt Jean sent him to check on us." Nova smiled wryly.

"To make sure we weren't making out in the cemetery?"

"That's weird. But yes. That's probably exactly why she sent him."

"Great."

Ethan followed her around the house. The horses were in the yard, munching on grass, their reins dragging on the ground. Justin stood about ten feet from them with Sonny.

When he saw them approaching, he picked up Doc's reins and handed them to Ethan. "Remind me to show you how to tie up a horse."

"Yeah. That would be great," Ethan said sheepishly.

He stuck his foot in the stirrup, swung his leg over, and settled into the saddle.

Nova retrieved Marilyn's reins from the ground. Marilyn nuzzled her and stood perfectly still while she climbed into the saddle. She leaned forward and laid her head on the mare's neck.

"I really want to take you home," Nova whispered.

Marilyn tossed her head as if in agreement.

"Everybody ready?" Justin didn't wait for an answer before he turned Sonny and headed into the woods. "This is a shortcut."

It was a narrow trail that cut through a particularly dense patch of trees and underbrush. The only way they could make it through was single file. Occasionally, a low-hanging branch smacked Nova in the face.

She picked a pine needle out of her mouth. "Is this payback for almost losing the horses?"

"Never even crossed my mind." Justin laughed.

They emerged from the woods into a field that bordered the paddocks next to the barn. When the horses were cleaned up and in their stalls, munching on hay, Nova and Ethan headed to the house.

Thirty minutes later, Nova emerged from her room, freshly washed and wearing a clean pair of shorts with a button-up blouse. Ethan wasn't in the kitchen when she entered, but everyone else was seated at the table. Stew had been loaded into bowls and set on plates, and there were baskets of cornbread at each end.

"Where's that boyfriend of yours?" Grandma Kate asked, smiling. Daniel was seated beside her, and she seemed to glow with a youthful radiance.

Nova stared, marveling at her transformation.

"Nova, honey, did you hear me?" Kate asked.

"Oh, yeah, sorry. I'll go check on him."

She darted up the stairs and knocked on the guest room that Aunt Jean called the "Old Fart Room." There was no response. She knocked again, and a disheveled Ethan opened the door wearing boxers and no shirt. Nova swallowed what felt like a lump of dough and tried to think of what to say while a familiar rush of blood colored her cheeks.

"I fell asleep. Did I miss dinner?"

"Almost. We're having it now. In the kitchen... downstairs." *What's wrong with me!* She blushed even harder.

"I know where the kitchen is, hot girl. Just give me a sec to get dressed." He gave her a smug look. "Want to come in and watch?"

"Oh my God, Ethan." Nova turned on her heel and marched down the hall to the stairs, feeling as though she wanted to crawl in a hole.

Five minutes later, Ethan strode into the kitchen and apologized for being late.

Aunt Jean waved as if brushing away the apology. "That's all right, honey. You've had a long day. Have a seat beside Nova. Maybe you can figure out why she's red as a beet. We can't get it out of her."

Ethan nudged Nova, who was doing her best to become invisible. "I think we both got some sun today, don't you?"

Nova nodded and shoved a huge bite of cornbread into her mouth. The whole table broke up laughing.

After dinner, Kate and Daniel took a walk while everyone else sat on the porch.

Ethan whispered in Nova's ear, "Do you want to go to the gazebo?"

"I can hardly hold my eyes open. Sorry."

"It's okay. I'll walk you up to your room."

Nova glanced at Aunt Jean. She was watching them with a knowing expression.

"Nova, you look beat. Why don't you run on up to bed?" Aunt Jean said. "Ethan can go down to the barn with

Justin and Marshall to lock up. Marshall will need someone to walk back to the house with him."

"Sure," Ethan said, obviously disappointed.

"Oh, I almost forgot. You and I are going into Charlotte tomorrow morning to get your stitches out. We should have gone when you first got here, but I couldn't get you in before now."

Going to a doctor's office in Charlotte was the last thing Nova wanted to do tomorrow. "I thought they were supposed to dissolve. I can barely feel them now."

"Maybe they did, but your mom said you have to follow up with a doctor. Don't worry, honey. We won't be gone but a couple of hours. I'm sure Justin will keep Ethan busy."

"Great." Nova sighed, not liking this new development at all.

She headed up to her room, changed, and crawled into bed. As much as she wanted to be with Ethan, she felt as if she'd been up for days. She needed to sleep. It didn't take long for the sounds of the garden to lull her to the threshold of sleep. It was the same every night—a familiar lullaby just for her. Nova let herself drift off into that warm, comfortable place.

Sometime later, a light tapping on her door roused her. Had she dreamed it? Then it started again, followed by a rustling sound. She slipped out of bed and tiptoed to her door. The faint light through the window illuminated the room just enough for her to see that someone had slid something under her door. She retrieved it and flipped on the lamp by her bed. It was a note.

Meet me at the gazebo at midnight. Ethan

Nova climbed back into bed. The clock on the bedside table read 10:32 p.m. Almost an hour and a half to wait. She closed her eyes and tried to relax, but it was no use.

She'd barely eaten any dinner, and her stomach was growling.

She slipped out of bed again and grabbed a pair of jeans from the chest. Everyone here seemed to be up every day at the crack of dawn, so hopefully they were all in bed now. When she stepped into the kitchen, her aunt was sitting in the armchair at the kitchen table, sipping on a cup of hot chocolate.

"I had a feeling I might see you."

Nova's mouth fell open. "How?"

"Honey, if you ate two bites of dinner, I'd be surprised." She laughed. "Don't be embarrassed. I was young and in love once."

The pot was keeping warm on the stove, and there was an empty cup and a bag of marshmallows next to it. Nova poured herself a cup, added the marshmallows, and plopped down next to Aunt Jean. Neither of them said anything at first.

Finally Nova asked something that had been bothering her since her first night back in this timeline. "When I traveled in the tapestry… why didn't you know it?"

"I've been thinking about that, and the more I mull it over, the more it makes sense. I think when you travel back and forth in a specific timeline, it's like changing the course of a river—like building a dam to make the water take a completely different path."

Nova couldn't help smiling. "You and your analogies."

"I know, I know. Matthew used to tease me about that all the time. But I like them. They make it easier to see the big picture."

"I like them too," Nova said.

"Okay then. Like I said, if you change the way the water flows, it's natural that other people on the river—other *travelers*—are going to notice. You're changing their course too. But when you're in the tapestry and you want to enter a different river, you slip your canoe in and let the water pull you along on the same course. You're not changing anything, at least not at first. It makes sense that no one would notice another canoe just going along with the current."

"I guess that makes sense. Still…"

"It's confusing, isn't it—this power we have?"

"Definitely," Nova agreed.

"One thing I've learned over the years is that it is what it is. If you try to understand everything, you'll go crazy."

Nova impulsively hugged her aunt. "I'm glad we have this gift though. Aren't you?"

Aunt Jean smiled. "I sure am."

***

Nova sat on the window seat and breathed in the scent of the garden. She still had thirty minutes to wait before meeting Ethan at the gazebo. She'd been relieved when her aunt had accompanied her upstairs because they could never have slipped past her in the kitchen at midnight. She watched the clock click off another minute that seemed more like five. The four-poster was inviting, but she didn't want to fall asleep. Instead, she laid her head on the windowsill and closed her eyes. *Just for a few minutes…*

Nova jolted awake and looked at the clock. It read a quarter after twelve. She jumped up, her heart pounding. He must think she wasn't coming! She slipped out the door and ran lightly down the hall and down the stairs. The light was on over the stove. Even so, she stubbed her toe on the armchair at the end of the table. She had to clamp her hand over her mouth to keep from crying out.

She let herself out the door to the veranda and ran down the path to the gazebo. He wasn't there. Nova collapsed on the steps, horribly disappointed.

"I was beginning to wonder if you were coming, hot

girl."

Nova wheeled around as he came down the steps and sat beside her. "Where were you? You weren't there a second ago!"

"I hid behind one of the big chairs when I heard what sounded like a large person charging through the garden." He laughed. "You weren't exactly quiet, you know. I had to be sure it was you."

"Oh my God. I didn't know I was making that much noise."

"Trust me."

"Okay then. If we only have a couple of minutes before someone finds us, there's something I want to do."

"What's tha—"

Nova's lips met his before he had a chance to finish. He wrapped his arms around her and kissed her back—passionately. When they came up for air, they were both breathless.

"Can we meet here every night?" he asked, grinning.

"Ha! We'll see." Nova kissed him again, softly this time. "You know I'm gonna travel again. You understand that, right?"

"Yeah, I do," he said seriously. "I wish you didn't have to."

"I know."

"I guess what I really wish is that I could go with you."

Nova thought about the time she'd traveled at Ethan's house and he'd felt something. Was it possible that he'd reacted as a traveler would? Or had it just been a coincidence? Maybe everyone had the ability to travel in time but they didn't know. Maybe somewhere in the past, one of the Grants had figured it out, and from that time on, their family had honed the gift, generation after generation.

She looked at Ethan and decided that it was better to let it go. "I wish I could take you with me. It just doesn't work that way."

"At least we have the whole summer." Ethan's voice was strained.

"Yes. We have the summer." That was a lie. Nova looked away.

"Hey," Ethan whispered, sounding on edge. "Listen…"

They heard voices coming from the veranda, and Nova took his hand.

"Come this way," she said quietly.

She led him around the gazebo and cut through the back side of the garden. They made their way to the barn, then stole silently up the hill to the house. Nova tried the door into the kitchen, but it was locked.

"Okay, hot girl. What now?"

She put her finger to her lips and listened. They could still hear the voices.

"I think that's my grandmother and Justin's grandfather," she whispered.

"What are they doing out this time of night?" Ethan said a little too loudly.

Nova shot him a hard look. "Probably the same thing we're doing," she mouthed almost silently.

He looked sheepish. "Right. That's nice… and a little gross."

She jabbed him in the stomach as they heard laughter followed by the sound of the veranda door closing.

"Oh my God. He's staying in Justin's apartment!" she said frantically.

Ethan looked toward the barn and back at her. "He'll be walking right past us."

"Yes! Crap! Come on." Nova grabbed Ethan's hand and took off toward the front of the house.

With a nearly full moon, it would be easy enough to see them running in the shadows, but there was nothing they could do about that. She was afraid to look back.

"Why is this freaking house so big?" Ethan asked breathlessly.

When they reached the corner, they ducked behind the wall and peered around in time to see Daniel was almost to the barn.

"He had to have seen us," Ethan stated matter-of-factly.

"Maybe not." Nova hoped that was the case.

"You're kidding, right?"

"Whatever. Let's go back in. I hope Grandma Kate didn't lock us out."

They walked around the house to the back and across the veranda. When Nova tried the door, it opened easily. "Thank God."

They stepped inside and looked around to make sure Kate had gone upstairs to her room.

"All clear." Ethan sounded relieved. He pulled her into another kiss.

Nova pulled away. "We have to get upstairs."

"That works for me." He grinned.

"To our *separate* rooms." She giggled.

Ethan clutched his chest and pretended to be wounded. At the top of the stairs, he took her hand and kissed it. "Tomorrow."

Nova smiled. "Tomorrow."

She fell into bed, still smiling. A gentle rain was falling, and she listened to the soft patter through the open window. This had been a perfect night. She closed her eyes and drifted off, imagining a whole summer of nights like this.

CHAPTER 15

"Nova! Nova! Get up!" It was Alana, impatient as usual. "Get up, little sister. You have to see this!"

Nova pulled the covers over her head and tried to shake off the cruel dream. Just a few hours ago, she'd been with Ethan at the gazebo. Why couldn't she dream about that?

"I'm serious! Get up!"

Her sister couldn't be calling out to her. Allie was gone. In this timeline, she'd died as a newborn.

But the dream refused to shut down. "Nova! I'm giving you one minute, and then I'm bringing the ice bucket!"

Something was wrong. This dream didn't feel like a dream at all. Nova threw the covers back and sat up. Nausea hit her even before she had the words out. "Allie—how?"

"Surprise!" Alana jumped on the bed, beaming. "Can you believe we're here?"

Nova felt the contents of her stomach threatening to come up any second. "Oh my God..." was all she could manage to get out.

She gripped the covers with both hands and held her breath, willing her brain to slow down so she could comprehend what had happened. She was certain she hadn't traveled, at least not on purpose. Had she done something unconsciously?

Alana grabbed her shoulders. "What's wrong with you? Are you sick?"

"What happened?" Nova's voice was barely audible.

"You didn't think I could pull something like this off, did you?" Alana laughed.

Nova's heart nearly pounded out of her chest. "Oh my God. What did you do?"

Alana ignored her. "This place is awesome. You have to get up!"

Nova squeezed her eyes shut and searched for the thread back to Willow Hill, but there was absolutely no connection. She wasn't the one who'd done this, so there was no way to go back.

Alana pursed her lips. "What's wrong with you? You look catatonic."

Nova stared at her sister, speechless. She had no idea where they even were. Her brain struggled to take in the unfamiliar surroundings. They were in a large, elegant bedroom. There were two beds with matching upholstered head and footboards. The beds were separated by a delicate, marble-topped table and lamp. An ornately carved armoire stood on the opposite wall next to a floral-fabric-covered chaise lounge. Lights twinkled faintly overhead from a gilded crystal chandelier, washed out by the sunlight streaming in through open glass-paned doors that led to a wrought-iron-enclosed balcony. Nova heard the bustling sounds of a city but had no idea where she was.

Alana skipped out onto the balcony and leaned slightly over the rail. "Come look!"

Nova scooted to the end of her bed and peered through the French doors at the Eiffel Tower. "Oh my God." She felt a fresh wave of nausea. "We're in Paris. Allie, what did you do?"

"Pretty cool, huh? You're not the only traveler in the family, you know." Alana beamed.

"But I was… you were…" Nova shook her head

violently, trying to clear it. How was this even possible? She should have been back in a timeline where her sister was dead.

"I knew you were gonna duck out of the trip, so I brought us ahead. To Paris." Alana was clearly pleased with herself.

"But how?"

"What aren't you getting, little sister? I traveled! What's wrong with you? You're supposed to know how this works."

"When did you do this?"

"Last night. Well, I guess not *technically* last night. I just aimed for us waking up in Paris, and here we are! I brought us forward, just like you did before. I didn't plan it very well though. I think we're on our last day here."

"Oh my God. You don't know what you've done! I was back at Aunt Jean's."

"Aunt Jean's? When did you go there?" Alana frowned.

"After I came into your room to say good night." Nova felt as if the room was closing in. It was hard to breathe. Just hours ago, she'd been with Ethan at Willow Hill. Now she was apparently in the same timeline she'd switched out of, which meant Marshall was gone again. Nova burst into tears. "You don't know what you've done. I'm not supposed to be here."

Alana set her jaw. "Let me get this straight. You're upset that we're in Paris, in an awesome apartment, with a view of *that!*" She pointed at the Eiffel Tower.

"You don't understand." Nova wiped her eyes on the bedsheet.

Alana planted herself on the end of the bed, arms crossed. "Okay. Make me understand."

Nova took a deep breath and let it out slowly. "There's something I didn't tell you before."

"Okay. So tell me now," she said, obviously fuming.

"And it better be good because we're in freaking Paris and you don't even care. And while you're at it, tell me why on earth you were supposedly at Aunt Jean's? I don't remember any plan to go back. I'm guessing you traveled there. Why? What's this weird obsession you have with Willow Hill?"

"Allie…" Nova struggled to collect her thoughts, unsure whether telling her sister about Marshall was a good idea. But how else could she make her understand?

"Still waiting," Alana said, impatiently tapping her foot against the bedframe.

Nova looked her sister in the eye. "Do you remember me coming in to say good night last night? Or the night you––"

"I remember. That's why I did it. I could tell something was up."

"I thought you were asleep."

"Faking it. Duh." Alana kept tapping her foot on the frame. It was maddening.

"Can you please stop that?"

"Stop what? Oh." The tapping stopped.

"Allie… this is probably gonna sound bad to you, but I had a reason. A really important reason."

Alana's expression changed from angry to alarmed. "What did you do?"

Nova swallowed hard. "I traveled back to the timeline before… the one I was in when you were––"

"Dead?" Alana's voice was strained. "Why? What did I do?"

Nova threw her arms around her sister. "You didn't do anything! It wasn't because of you!"

Alana pushed her away. "But after getting me back, you decided you liked it better without me!"

Nova couldn't blame her for being angry. If the situation were reversed, she'd probably have been screaming by now.

"Of course not!" Nova said emphatically. "I *had* to go

back! And I was going to save you again, I swear!"

It was Alana's turn to burst into tears. "So that's why you don't like being here in Paris? It's not Paris that's wrong. It's me."

"Oh my God. This isn't coming out like it's supposed to." Nova couldn't bear her sister thinking she'd abandoned her or worse. "I had to go back for Marshall! When I went forward in time and brought you back, I lost him. It was like he never existed."

"So you knocked me off again to go back for some guy?" Alana's grief turned back to anger.

"No! Not some guy." Nova took a deep breath. "Our nine-year-old brother."

Alana stopped crying and stared wide-eyed at Nova. She didn't even seem to be breathing.

Nova shook her head sadly. "I never wanted to tell you about Marshall. I knew how upset you'd be if you knew…"

"I was the reason he didn't get to live. That's what you're saying, right?"

"It wasn't your fault."

"No. But it was because of me." All the color had drained from her face.

"Listen, I know there's a way to have you both. There has to be. I wanted to go back and start over. When I brought you back, I did it by imagining us together on our birthdays. If it worked with you, that has to mean it would work again. I'll just imagine a future with you *and* Marshall."

"It can't be that simple."

"Maybe not. But I thought Aunt Jean could help me figure it out."

"Why do you need her? Let's do it now. Travel back… or forward. You can picture all of us back at home. Or better yet, here in Paris."

"There's a problem."

Alana frowned. "What?"

"You can't go backward or forward in this life and bring him back because he's not anywhere in this timeline. He never existed."

"Then how...?"

"I'm not sure, but I think I can use the tapestry."

Alana leaned forward. "What's the tapestry?"

"It's hard to explain." Nova hesitated, unsure whether or not to tell her reckless sister how to jump into countless timelines.

"Try," Alana said impatiently.

Nova collected her thoughts, her great-grandmother's word playing over and over in her head like before—*dangerous.* In the brief time Nova had known her sister, she'd figured out that Alana was probably the last Grant you'd ever want to give that power to. And yet, it was as much her right to know about the tapestry as it was Nova's.

"Well? Are you telling me or what?"

Nova looked down at her hands. "I don't know."

Alana was aghast. "You don't trust me?"

She looked up again. "I do trust you." But the truth was, she didn't trust her sister not to misuse the tapestry. Hadn't Nova done the same thing though? She'd jumped in with very little forethought. Her eyes met Alana's. "I'll tell you, but you have to promise not to use it unless we both agree. Okay?"

Alana scooted close to her on the bed. "Okay, little sister."

"I'm serious. Promise me."

"I promise."

Nova took a deep breath and let it out slowly. She was stalling, trying to figure out exactly how to describe the tapestry in a way that wouldn't make her sister want to plunge in right away.

"Nova..."

"Sorry. Okay... you know we're in a timeline right now?"

"Of course."

"And you know that you can travel back and forth in this life, right?"

"Yes, Nova. Get to it." Alana had resumed tapping the bedframe with her foot.

"Stop tapping, please."

She stopped. "Sorry. You're making me nervous. Like something bad's about to happen."

"Nothing bad will happen if we're smart and don't rush into traveling again."

Alana nodded.

"Okay. This is one timeline. When I was at Aunt Jean's, that was another timeline. And the one where Dad was killed on the bridge was a different one. There are lots of timelines that are possible. The tapestry is where they all are—all your timelines and mine... every traveler. There are thousands of them. Evelyn Grant, our great-grandmother, wrote about it in her journal, but she didn't say how to get there."

Alana was hanging on her every word. "How do you know for sure it exists then?"

"I saw it."

Alana's eyes lit up. "You did?"

"Yes. I've been there. It's incredible. All of your timelines weave in and out of other travelers' timelines. It's amazing. It looks like sort of like a giant, elaborate spider web. Except there's no pattern to it. And they all glow silver with slightly different hues. It's more beautiful than you can imagine."

"How do you get there?"

That was the question Nova had been dreading, because once she shared the process of finding the tapestry there would be no taking it back.

"Nova! Tell me how to get there," Alana prodded.

"If I tell you, will you promise not to go there unless we both agree?"

"Why?"

"Because it's dangerous. Evelyn didn't even tell her daughters how to find it for that reason. And she wrote that in her journal—that it was best to leave it alone. I've been there, and I can tell you it's easy to get caught up in the different lives. It's like they want to suck you in. If you're not careful, you could end up somewhere you don't really want to be. And you can lose people you love."

"I'd be careful."

"It's not just a matter of being careful," Nova said. "It does something to you that makes you almost forget why you're there. And then it won't leave you alone."

"What do you mean?"

"I mean I still feel it—the connection to the tapestry. It didn't bother me at first. I figured it would go away. But even now, if I think about it, I can feel it."

"That doesn't sound so bad. I still want to see it."

"I know you do. But we need to wait until we can talk to Grandma Kate. She's been there too."

"Grandma Kate doesn't want to have anything to do with us."

"That's not true. I talked to her in the other timeline, and she told me a lot about the tapestry."

Alana shook her head. "Weird. I haven't seen her in years."

"Yeah, I know. We can talk about that later."

"Okay. So, your plan is for us to go to the tapestry, and that's how we'll find another timeline with Marshall. Is that right?"

"That's right."

She perked up. "Okay, little sister. We agree we're going to the tapestry eventually, right?"

"Well... *I* am."

"Fine. But you're not going right now. Not until we can get advice from our grandmother. Am I straight on that?"

"Maybe. I don't know how hard it'll be to get her to

open up this time."

"Details, details. You'll figure it out. All I need to know is that you're not doing anything *right now*. Would you say that's accurate?"

"Yeah. I'd say so."

"Okay then! If you want me to go along with the whole waiting thing and being dead thing and whatever else you have in mind while you try to fix this mess, I want one day in Paris. Just one. That's all we'd get anyway since I've landed us on our last full day here. So I want you and me to see as much of this incredibly awesome place as we possibly can in one day. Agreed?"

"What about Mom and Dad?"

Alana smiled. "They're gone the whole day."

"Where?"

"Dad has another book signing. Can you believe it? He left a note reminding us. Of course, it wasn't really *reminding* since we just got here, but…"

"Get used to it. Happens to me all the time." Nova gave her a wry smile.

Alana ignored her comment, busy with her own thoughts. "It's weird how famous Dad is. I can't get it in my head."

"Yeah. The flight attendant saved his plastic cup."

"What flight attendant?"

Nova shook her head. "Never mind." She looked out the doors of the balcony at the Eiffel Tower. "We definitely have to go there."

Alana followed her gaze and grinned. "Right, little sister."

"Okay. One day in Paris. Just you and me. And no traveling. Agreed?"

"One day." Alana threw her arms around Nova. "And you can't talk about it being only one day, or it'll ruin the whole thing."

"I promise.

CHAPTER 16

"What are we supposed to use for money?" Nova asked.

"Dad said to take what we need out of the drawer in their room."

Alana grabbed Nova's hand and pulled her out into the hall and across the living area to their parents' room. Nova was nervous that her parents could still be in the apartment, but her fears were unfounded. Alana yanked open dresser drawers. When she came across the right one, she sucked in a breath and pulled the drawer all the way out.

Nova looked inside and gasped. "Holy crap. How much is that?"

Alana shrugged. "No idea. It's French money. It could be a thousand dollars or twenty bucks."

"Well, how much should we take?"

"All of it."

"Are you kidding? What if it's all they have for the trip?"

"Nova. Dad is at some big book signing... *in Paris.* You think this is all the money he has?"

"Oh. Right. They can probably get more if they need it."

Alana grabbed the wad of cash and stuffed it in her purse. "We have to get the key from the little old French lady on the first floor."

"What key?"

"The key to the apartment. Dad said she has an extra key and we're supposed to get it if we leave. I would've gotten it before, but we're on the sixth floor."

"So?"

"The elevator is like a coffin, and I didn't feel like walking down and back up again."

"How long were you awake before me?" Nova laughed.

"It didn't take that long to read a note and see the elevator." Alana was already pulling on jeans. "Anyway, she's the key guardian or something."

"Who?"

"Pay attention! The old woman on the first floor. Her apartment is right by the door."

"The elevator looks like a coffin?"

"Focus! What's wrong with you? We have to hurry!"

"Why do we have to hurry?"

"I have one day in Paris, and I have a list of everywhere I want to go. Not that we'll get to all of them, but—" Alana looked as if she was about to burst into tears.

Nova gave her a quick hug. "We'll come back, okay? I promise."

Alana collected herself. "I know. I trust you."

Nova pulled on jeans and a silk button-up blouse. "Do I look French?" She grinned.

Alana laughed. "Sure. Why not?" She grabbed a sweater from the closet. "It might get chilly later."

Nova picked up the note that was lying on Alana's bed and read the first sentence. "We can't let Mom and Dad beat us back here. We'd be grounded forever!"

"Why is that?"

"He said to stay on this street. We're only supposed to get food and come right back."

"Oh my God." Alana snatched the paper from her hands and tossed it on the bed. "What difference does it make? We're leaving this timeline."

"Not today."

"It doesn't matter. Say we travel in a few days. They can ground us for a month, or a year, or the rest of our freaking lives. It won't matter."

"Sorry. You're right."

Alana located a sweater in Nova's suitcase and shoved it at her. "I don't want to come back here if you get cold."

"How will we lock the door if we don't have the key from…?"

"Madame Marinier."

"Good grief. How long was that note?"

Alana laughed. "You know Dad. He believes in details."

"One of us will have to come back and lock up."

"Not me."

"You're ridiculous. The elevator can't be that bad."

They stepped into the hall and pulled the door closed. The elevator was directly across the hall, and Alana had been right. There was barely enough room for the both of them.

Nova gasped. "I take it back…"

"Told you."

"I'm not getting on that thing."

"Me either."

The stairway spit them out in the tiny foyer of the apartment building. Madame Marinier's apartment was the first one on the left upon entering the building.

Alana cautiously knocked on her door and waited. Several minutes passed before Alana knocked again, a little louder this time. The door sprang open immediately, and there stood an elderly woman who couldn't have been more than four and a half feet tall. She wore a buttoned flowered dress and a kerchief on her head. In her hand was a feather duster, posed as if she planned to defend herself if need be.

"Madame Marinier?" Alana choked out.

"*Oui,*" she answered sternly. "*Qu'est-ce que tu veux?*"

"Umm—we need a key for 602." Alana had raised her voice to a decibel level that made the woman step backward and raise the feather duster menacingly.

Nova leaned toward Alana and whispered, "Why are you yelling? She's not deaf."

Madame Marinier's eyes darted to Nova, and her expression changed to amusement. "Americans," she huffed, abruptly closing the door.

"What do we do now?" Alana whispered.

Before Nova could respond, the door jerked open again. Madame Marinier stuck her hand out to Nova. In it was a key. Nova gave her a warm smile and took it.

"Merci!" Alana gushed, still too loudly.

The old woman gave her a harsh look and closed the door with a resounding thud.

"What's wrong with you? Yelling at someone doesn't suddenly make them understand another language."

Alana shrugged and pulled a map out of her pocket.

"Where'd you get that?" Nova asked.

"It was in the drawer with the money." Alana grinned.

"Who's going up to lock the door?"

Alana stood her ground. "Not me."

Nova sighed. "Fine. I'll go." She darted up the stairs and locked the apartment door, then sprinted down again.

Alana stood at the double doors that led out to the street. "Why are you out of breath?"

"Funny. You can return the key when we get back."

"That woman is scary. I don't think she likes me."

"Maybe if you don't yell at her..."

"Okay, but if I go missing you'll know where to look."

"She's at least a foot shorter than you are. I don't think you have to worry."

Once outside, Alana pointed out the bright blue double doors into the apartment building. "We have to remember where we are so we can get back. I don't see any other blue doors on this street, so that'll help."

Nova scanned the area around their apartment. There was a restaurant with red awnings right next door and a pastry shop just beyond that. A wonderful aroma filled the air. "We should get something to eat, don't you think?"

"That works for me. I don't think I could resist that smell even if I wanted to." Alana laughed.

They bought chocolate croissants in the pastry shop. Alana stumbled through the process of figuring out exactly how much to give the amused young woman behind the counter.

When they were back outside, Alana stuffed the change into her purse and shook her head. "I have no idea if I gave her the right amount. We may have just spent fifty dollars on two croissants."

Nova took a bite out of hers and mumbled, "Oh my God. This is amazing."

Alana stuffed hers down and dug the map out of her purse again. "We need to head west on Rue de l'Université." She looked around to get her bearings. "I think that's this way."

"The Eiffel Tower is *right there*. Why do we need the map?"

"Oh. Right." Alana giggled, folding the map before putting it back in her purse.

"We're on Avenue Rapp."

"How do you know?"

Nova pointed at a sign. "See?"

They turned onto Rue de l'Université and made their way along the busy sidewalk as people bustled in both directions. These were obviously Parisians, or at least seasoned travelers, because not one of them seemed impressed by the huge steel tower looming overhead. They turned right onto Avenue de la Bourdonnais and left back onto Rue de l'Université.

"These roads are confusing." Alana pulled out the map again. "Weren't we just on this one?"

"It doesn't matter. Look." Nova felt the hairs on the back of her neck stand up.

The elaborately sculpted ironwork was even more impressive as they approached and stood underneath the massive structure. It certainly looked solid enough, but that fact did little to quell her fear.

"I'm not promising I'll go all the way to the top," Nova said.

Alana grabbed her arm. "You have to!"

She dragged Nova through the crowd to the east pillar to buy tickets, which amounted to Alana holding up a small wad of cash and the person at the counter taking most of it.

"Do you have any idea how much you're paying for things, or are you just hoping everyone we give money to is honest?" Nova was worried that Alana would give away all their money and they'd be stranded while their oblivious parents enjoyed a late dinner in some fancy restaurant, unaware that their daughters were wandering the streets of Paris penniless.

"Don't worry. There's plenty left."

"Not the point. This isn't even our money!"

Alana ignored Nova's comment and pulled her into the mass of people waiting for the first lift up. They seemed to have stumbled onto a group of befuddled tourists milling around instead of forming a line for the elevator. When it arrived and the doors flew open, the crowd poured in like a tsunami, barely giving the people getting off a chance to get out of the way.

Nova pulled her sister out of harm's way just in time. "I say we wait for the next one."

Alana nodded vigorously.

When the next one came, they climbed aboard and

rode to the second level. The boisterous crowd had apparently taken the elevator up to the top, as there were only five or six others on that level. Relieved, they took advantage of the relative quiet and surveyed the area. From this vantage point, they had an expansive view of the Seine, with its bridges that took vehicles and pedestrians between the east and west banks.

The entire city of Paris was laid out before them.

"This is incredible," Alana said.

"*Oui, incroyable!*" said a young woman standing behind them. She had a small child who seemed mesmerized by the two American teenagers.

"I'm sorry. I don't speak French," Nova apologized.

"It is all right. You are American, *oui*?"

"Yes." Nova looked to her sister for help, but Alana was already standing at the elevator to go on up.

"Are you enjoying your time in Paris?" the woman asked.

Nova turned back to her and smiled. "Yes, so far. We haven't been here long."

The little girl looked to be about four or five years old. She pointed at Alana and asked in a tiny voice, "*Est-elle ta soeur?*"

Nova looked at her mother, who smiled and said, "She wants to know if she is your sister."

"Yes. My twin sister."

As her mother translated, the little girl seemed surprised, looking back and forth between Nova and Alana. "*Elle ne te ressemble pas.*"

Her mother said something else to her, then apologized. "I'm sorry. She said that you don't look like your sister. I explained that not all twins look alike."

Alana waved for Nova to come on as the elevator to the upper level opened.

"Enjoy your day, *mademoiselle*. You must sit on the Champs de Mars this evening. You will see the lights come on. It is quite beautiful."

"The Champs de Mars?"

"It is the park you see down there. Many people come to see the tower when it lights up every evening."

"Thank you." Nova smiled again. "We'll do that."

The little girl smiled and waved goodbye as Nova hurried over to the elevator. Alana grabbed her hand as they stepped on.

"What was that all about?" Alana laughed.

"She was nice," Nova said as she stared at the surrounding landscape retreating beneath them. "This is really high up."

"It's fantastic! We can see everything! Just imagine what it'll look like from the top."

Nova envied her sister's confidence. In the brief time they'd known each other, Nova had learned that the little girl who had jumped fearlessly into the pool when she was five was still alive and well at sixteen.

"This is high enough, Allie."

"I paid to go to the top. So, we're going. It'll be great. Trust me, little sister."

Nova reluctantly climbed onto another elevator and closed her eyes, refusing to look even as Alana gasped in delight at the view.

"You can't miss this. Please! It's incredible."

Nova sucked in her breath, opened her eyes, and looked around. The city lay before them in all of its magnificence. Not a single photo or painting she had ever seen even came close to the real thing. "It's so beautiful."

Alana smiled. "Told you."

The woman with the little girl exited the elevator beside them. "I see you made it all the way to the top."

"Yes! It's wonderful," Nova answered breathlessly. "I'm still trying to get used to being this high up though." She turned her attention to the little girl, who seemed completely at ease. "You're not afraid of heights?"

As her mother translated, the little girl shook her head.

"Sophie loves to come here," her mother said proudly. "She is not afraid of anything."

"Sounds like someone I know." Nova elbowed Alana playfully.

Alana leaned down to Sophie. "My sister worries so I don't have to."

Nova stuck her tongue out at her sister, and the child giggled.

"You can see so much of Paris from here," the woman said, obviously proud of her city. "I think you girls would be particularly interested in les Champs-Élysées. There are so many wonderful stores."

"That settles it," Alana declared. "We're going there next."

Alana pulled Nova, who was as reluctant to leave as she had been to reach the top, onto the next elevator, and Sophie waved as the elevator doors closed.

They followed the map across the Pont D'Alma Bridge to Metro line 9. After one stop, they changed to line 1—Franklin D. Roosevelt.

"We need to get off at the George V. It looks like that's where most of the shops are!" Alana wasn't even trying to hide her excitement. If she had worn a giant TOURIST sign on her head, she wouldn't have been more obvious.

Nova once again admired her sister's enthusiasm for life and wished she possessed the same exuberance.

They exited the metro at the George V station and stepped onto the Champs-Élysées in all of its grandeur. The atmosphere was electric with so many people milling about the sprawling sidewalks.

"Let's go there first." Alana pointed toward a shop that seemed to be attracting quite a crowd.

The sign over the door read "Ladurée." They stepped

inside and gasped. Several patrons turned to stare at them, and Nova felt her face turn red. Alana obviously couldn't have cared less that they'd just announced their entrance in such an undignified manner.

"This is amazing!" she whispered a little too loudly. "I've never seen so many different pastries. Oh my God, look at the chocolate ones!"

Nova heard someone ahead of them snicker.

Alana continued gushing over their culinary good fortune. "I'm suddenly starving. Let's get one of everything!"

Nova laughed. "Maybe not *everything*. We do have to eat some normal food at some point too."

"We're in Paris. There aren't any rules, little sister." Alana reached into her purse and pulled out another wad of cash. After selecting three pastries each, she held up the money and the man behind the counter took most of it.

Nova shook her head. "I think I need to be in charge of the money from now on."

"Stop worrying. We have plenty left."

"I'd feel better if I knew how much we'd already spent."

They continued down the boulevard, stepping into store after store. Alana was in heaven, but after a while, Nova needed a break. She sat on a bench while her sister entered yet another shop. As Nova waited, watching people stroll by, it suddenly hit her—she had seen this exact bench in one of her timelines in the tapestry. But in that life, she'd been sitting with her dad while Celeste and Alana shopped. They had walked out of the store Alana was in right now, laden with packages. Nova could still visualize the scene. Maybe this was actually that timeline. Maybe earlier in their trip, she'd sat on this same bench with her dad while her mom and sister shopped.

Nova felt a chill go up her spine. Did the tapestry *know* every choice you'd make? Every outcome? But this hadn't been *her* choice. It was Alana's. Nova felt her brain trying to wrap itself around the idea that the tapestry somehow had control over her life. She closed her eyes and tried to shut out the sounds around her. And there it was. The almost imperceptible tug. *Oh my God... I can feel it still.*

CHAPTER 17

Alana plopped down on the bench beside her. "Are you catatonic again? I said your name, like, five times."

"I'm s-sorry."

Alana's expression turned serious. "Is everything okay?"

"Sure. It's fine. I'm just tired of shopping."

"Yeah. What's up with that? We used to shop for hours."

Nova looked at her sister with tears in her eyes. "I never had a sister to shop with."

Alana said nothing for a moment, then put her arm around her. "Sometimes I forget you don't remember." She laid her head on Nova's shoulder. "To tell the truth, I mostly dragged you along with me. You never liked it that much. You were being a good sister. Didn't Mom ever take you?"

"She wanted me to go with her, but I guess it wasn't fun for me. I always wanted to find what I needed and get out of there."

"You're weird. I love to shop. Maybe they switched babies at the hospital and our *real* twins are out there somewhere, one of them *much* better dressed than the other." Alana giggled and pretended to jab her in the side.

Nova laughed. "That would explain a lot."

"So no more shopping, huh?"

"No more shopping. Sorry."

"It's okay. We're almost out of money anyway." Alana had several bags on the bench. "I think you may be right about people ripping us off."

"Great. How are we gonna explain the missing money?"

Alana cocked her head. "It doesn't matter. Remember?"

"Oh, right. So why did you buy the clothes? You won't get to wear them."

Alana's face fell. "You're right." She shook her head. "You could've mentioned that about two hours ago."

Nova looked at her watch. "It's almost five thirty."

"Where do you want to go next?"

"Maybe the Louvre?"

"Ooooo… a *museum?*"

"A very famous museum. Don't you want to see the *Mona Lisa?*"

"Oh, yes. Please. Let's go."

"Don't be sarcastic."

"Sorry. We can go if you want to." Alana pulled out the map again. "It's not that far."

"You know what I'd really like to do?"

"No, what?"

"Find someplace where we can get a hamburger and fries." Nova rubbed her stomach. "I'm starving."

"Yeah. No more bread or sweets." Alana looked around. "There are restaurants here, but I'm not sure we can afford them. They look expensive, and I've given most of our money away."

"Great. There's probably food back at the apartment."

"You're sure you don't want to see the famous boring-lady painting? I was really looking forward to that."

"I'm sure." Nova giggled.

They followed the map to a metro station next to the Place de la Concorde and got off at the Pont D'Alma Bridge. From there, they walked back to the apartment and let themselves in with the key they'd gotten from Madame Marinier. The refrigerator was stocked with cold cuts, cheese, and fruit, and there was a fresh baguette on the table. They made sandwiches and settled into the cushioned chairs on the balcony overlooking the tower.

"This is incredible," Alana mumbled, her mouth full.

"I'd still like a burger, but this works too."

"I can't believe it's over. You know… our trip."

Nova shoved the last bite in her mouth and stood. "It's still early. That woman at the tower this morning said we should go to the Champs de Mars."

"What woman?"

"The one with the little girl. What was her name? Sophie?"

"Oh yeah. She was cute." Alana was still sitting with her feet propped up on the iron railing.

Nova put her hands on her hips. "Did you hear what I said about going to the Champs de Mars?"

"I heard." Alana put the last bite of sandwich in her mouth.

"You know, it's not normal for me to be the eager one. That's supposed to be your job."

Alana laughed and jumped to her feet. "Really? You want to go back to the tower?"

"That's more like it."

"I was messing with you." Alana grinned. "We might get caught. Are you okay with that, Miss Perfect?"

Nova rolled her eyes. "Sure. But I don't think we'll get caught. Mom and Dad will probably be late. Just to be safe though, let's say we're back by nine o'clock."

"Nine it is." Alana grabbed her watch from the dresser in their room and fastened the clasp around her wrist. She pulled the map out of her purse and tried to open it while they skipped down the stairs.

"We don't need that. We're going to the park at the tower. I think it'll be easy to find."

"I'm using the map anyway, just in case."

"This is amazing. I finally found something you're afraid of." Nova laughed. "Getting lost."

"Yeah, well, Mom lost me at the mall once when we were little, and it scarred me for life." Alana pretended to swoon and almost fell down the last three steps. She grabbed Nova and nearly dragged her down too.

Madame Marinier peered out of her door as they stumbled past. "Hmpf!" she said before closing the door with a resounding thud.

"Great. She'll probably tell Dad about his unruly daughters," Nova fretted.

"No one can understand her," Alana pointed out.

"Allie, Dad speaks French."

"Oh yeah. Crap."

They followed the same route they'd taken that morning to the Eiffel Tower. The Parc du Champs de Mars was a sprawling expanse of grass teaming with people. Many had brought blankets to spread out while their children played. Couples, young and old, strolled along the walkway surrounding the park while a band played an assortment of decidedly French tunes at the far end.

A group of teenagers kicked around a soccer ball, but the activity seemed more about flirting than the game. One boy who looked about their age trotted over and tried to get them to join in.

Nova had the impression that Alana would have gladly gone with him, but Nova shook her head and found a spot on the grass to plop down. "I'm sorry, Allie. I'm thinking about Ethan, and we're leaving tomorrow anyway."

"It's okay." Alana lay back on the grass and looked at the tower. "He was cute though, don't you think? And that accent. Oh my God."

Nova pulled her sweater around her shoulders and chuckled. "Yeah. He was cute." She lay down beside her sister, content to be right there at that moment.

"You probably think you'll end up with Ethan, don't you?"

"I hope so."

"Yeah. Me too. You're perfect together."

"What about you and David?"

Alana didn't say anything for a long moment. When she spoke, her voice was uncharacteristically somber. "I doubt it. I like him, but so do lots of other girls. And that doesn't bother me. Not even a little. I think if he was the one, it would."

Nova thought about the ditzy twins at the party fawning all over Ethan. She'd been furious. "You'll meet someone. We're only sixteen."

"Nova?"

"Yeah?"

"I have so much I want to do. I want to go off to college. I want to travel and fall in love. I'm not ready to die."

"You're not gonna die. I'll find a timeline—"

"Stop," Alana interrupted. "You don't know that. And if you don't find one that has our brother and me both, what will you do?"

"I'll find one."

"But what if you don't?"

"I'll stay in the tapestry until I do."

"If it comes down to making a choice..." Alana swallowed back tears. "I want you to choose Marshall. I'm giving you *permission* to choose him."

"You're not gonna die. And neither is Marshall. I promise." Nova had no idea how to keep that promise. But no matter what happened, she never wanted to forget what if felt like to lie on the grass in the shadow of the Eiffel Tower next to her sister.

Neither of them said a word for at least half an hour. The band continued to play while everyone in the park went about their lives, unaware that everything could change in the blink of an eye. They weren't travelers. Nova envied them.

Finally, Alana broke the silence. "What time is it?"

"You're the one with the watch."

"Oh, right. It says eight forty-five."

"Why is it still so light? If we were home, it'd be getting dark by now."

"It's because of where we are on the planet. It doesn't get dark until later. I read it in the information section of my map."

Nova grinned. "You really love that map, don't you?"

Alana poked her shoulder with her fist. "Shut up."

"We won't make it back by nine."

Alana set her jaw. "I don't care. I want to see it."

Nova smiled. "Me too."

Just after nine thirty, the tower finally lit up. It was spectacular, as if millions and millions of fireflies had magically sprung from the steel. Nova had never seen anything so beautiful. A collective "ahh" rose up from the crowd.

Allie took Nova's hand and squeezed it. "Thanks for this, little sister."

CHAPTER 18

It was almost midnight when Dayton stuck his head through the doorway into their room. "What did you girls do today?" He seemed a little on edge.

Nova's throat went dry. She hated lying to her dad. "Not much."

He came the rest of the way into the room and closed the door. "Are you sure?"

Nova swallowed, for the second time, the chocolate truffle she'd just eaten. "Why?"

"When we pulled into the hotel where the event was held this morning, I got sick to my stomach and had a little vertigo. It passed after about thirty minutes, but I almost had to cancel the book signing. So I'm asking you again, did you do something while I was gone? Something that changed this timeline? Because that's exactly what it felt like. That's how I felt when you traveled at Aunt Jean's and we ended up back at home with Alana and no Marshall."

"I didn't travel."

"You swear? Not even a visit?"

"Yes, I swear I didn't travel, visit, or otherwise." She cleared her throat nervously as the truffle made another attempt to move up her esophagus. "But... Alana did."

"What? Alana traveled?" He was incredulous. "Why did you let her do that?"

"I didn't. She did it on her own. But that's not all."

Nova collected her thoughts, trying to determine how much she should tell him. "I just got here this morning, and so did Alana. She brought us here the night I came back from Grandma Kate's with Ethan."

Dayton's mouth hung open. He said nothing as he stared at her, dumbfounded. Finally, he practically fell trying to sit on the closest bed. "You got here today?"

"This morning."

"That's not possible. All we've done the last few weeks…"

Nova sat down beside him and put her hand on his arm. "You know it *is* possible. It's happened before."

He shook his head. "I knew something had happened, but this…"

"Alana jumped ahead to our trip, but she didn't focus on getting here when we had just arrived. So, here we are. The last day in Paris. Figures, huh?"

"And to think I decided to wait to change timelines until after the trip so you'd have that memory, even if it faded over time. We've been here over three weeks."

"We've been in Paris all this time?" Nova felt numb.

"No. We stayed here the first week. Mostly what we did was shop. Let me correct that. Mostly what we did was watch your mother and Alana shop." He laughed, but there was no humor in it. He sounded worn out. "I know where every bench in Paris is, especially on the Champs-Élysées."

"The bench! I saw us when I was—" She felt her heart nearly jump out of her chest. She'd almost said that she'd seen the two of them sitting on a bench while her mother and sister shopped. But Nova had seen that while she was in the tapestry, and she wasn't yet sure she wanted to tell him about that.

"What?" Dayton asked, sounding confused.

"Oh… I saw a bench when Allie and I went out to get food." It was a lame excuse for the slip up, and he obviously wasn't buying it.

"Is there something you're not telling me?" He frowned.

"It's nothing." She looked at her feet. This wasn't going well. She did her best to put on a believable smile. "Tell me what else we did on this trip."

Dayton eyed her suspiciously. "Tell me—what have you been up to?"

"Dad, I swear. This is not my doing." That much at least was true.

He didn't seem satisfied but continued on with the breakdown of their trip in spite of the tension between them. "Well, we can talk about it again later. Like I said, we were here the first week. My publisher knows the people who own this apartment. They're out of the country for nearly the whole summer and offered to let us stay here."

"That was nice," Nova said a little too enthusiastically.

Dayton studied her for a moment, frowning.

"Dad, come on."

He interpreted her anxiety as impatience. "Okay, sorry. This day has just been weird."

You said it! Nova had to fight the urge to laugh out loud. It wasn't at all funny, but her pent-up emotion had to come out some way, so her brain had decided to tweak the humor response. She bit her lip and focused on a stain on the rug under her feet.

"Why are you acting so strange?" Dayton asked irritably.

Nova looked up. "I didn't know I was." She still wanted to laugh. *What's wrong with me?* She cleared her throat again. "What did we do after the first week?"

Dayton sighed. "Fine. We took the train to Nice and rented a car so we could take day trips from there. That was your favorite part of the trip, except for Florence."

"So we went to Italy too." The urge to laugh was gone. Any moment she could break down and sob. It wasn't fair—not remembering. She was sorry she'd asked about the trip.

Dayton continued, unaware that every detail was like twisting a knife in her gut. "Yeah. After Nice, we went into Italy. Stopped at a few small towns and spent some time in Rome. Then back up to Florence. We were there two days. You and Alana loved it. Your mom did too. She wants to go back next summer. We stayed in a quaint little inn covered in vines. Our rooms opened up to a garden that Aunt Jean would've gone nuts over."

"It sounds amazing."

"It was." He noticed her expression and put his arm around her. "I'm so sorry, honey."

"It's not your fault. What did we do next? I want to know."

Dayton sighed. "After that, we went back to Nice, spent the night, then took a train back to Paris. I had a speaking engagement today, followed by a book signing and dinner with my publisher's contacts here. Tomorrow we head home."

Nova collapsed onto her bed and groaned. "I can't even express how bad it sucks that I don't remember any of that."

"I'll bet."

Alana came out of the bathroom wearing cutoffs and an oversized tee shirt, her hair in a towel. "What's wrong with you two? Did someone die?"

Nova sat up. "Dad was just telling me about the awesome trip we've had that we don't remember."

"Really?" Alana jumped on the end of Nova's bed excitedly. "Tell me!"

"I can't listen to this again." Nova grabbed the sweater draped across the end of Alana's bed and walked out to the balcony.

Alana joined her twenty minutes later. She sat in a cushioned wrought-iron chair and propped her feet against the balcony rail. The Eiffel Tower glittered against the night sky.

"It's beautiful, isn't it?" Alana sounded content, even happy.

"How are *you*, of all people, not bummed out? Did Dad tell you all we've done the past three weeks?"

"Yeah. Sounds like we had an awesome trip." Alana smiled. "Why are you so upset?"

Nova shook her head. "I'm upset because we missed it."

"Little sister, you're forgetting something amazing."

"What's that?"

Alana's smile deepened. "We can do it all again. As many times as we want to. We're time travelers."

Nova wanted to feel like her sister—like it would all be wonderful. But history had shown her that things didn't always work out the way you wanted them to. "You can't jump back and do things over and over. It doesn't work that way. The power doesn't last forever, and you can't waste it. And you can't know for sure what will happen when you go back. You might change something."

"I know. You told me all that before. But it's still wonderful to think we could travel again to the beginning of this trip and actually experience it. Just knowing that possibility is there… I guess that's enough. I couldn't stand it if I thought I'd never do it."

"I know. But this is the first time you've ever jumped forward. It's the first time you haven't remembered your past. And it's only the last three weeks. I've lost sixteen years of memories. I've lost my little brother and had to give you up after screwing things up so horribly. I still have that hanging over my head—the big question of how to have both you and Marshall. So our perspectives are different. I want to think everything will work out, that we'll travel and have this amazing life full of incredible experiences. It's just that, so far, a lot of it hasn't been so amazing."

Alana took her hand. "I hear you, little sister. But if we look at it that way, how will we ever have anything we want? We'll be too scared to try."

Nova felt as if she'd been slapped. Alana was right. Nova saw herself becoming like Grandma Kate—afraid of what *could* happen instead of embracing the possibility of what she could gain. Alana was hoping for wonderful. She wasn't worried about the other.

"I love you, Allie." Nova hugged her tightly. "You're right. We're gonna have an amazing life. And it starts with getting Marshall back."

Alana clapped her hand over her mouth to stifle a squeal. When she'd regained a semblance of control, she whispered, "Should we travel tonight?"

Nova shook her head. "There's something I have to do at home first. Do you mind?"

"No. We can wait 'til we get home. I think I know what the *something* is."

CHAPTER 19

They were up at five o'clock the next morning, packing and making last-minute travel arrangements for a ten o'clock flight. Celeste breezed around the apartment, straightening up and making sure they hadn't forgotten anything.

"You girls look under your beds. I found two pairs of shoes under mine."

"You're packing someone else's shoes?" Dayton winked at her.

"Very funny, Day. They're mine of course."

Dayton pulled open the money drawer. "Where's our cash?"

Nova and Alana held their breaths, waiting for the boom to be lowered.

"I have it," Celeste spoke up. She looked over her shoulder and winked at her daughters.

Dayton grabbed several bags and headed to the elevator. Celeste continued to pack, humming as she worked.

Nova cleared her throat. "Mom…"

"Hush. Your dad will be back any minute."

"But about the money—"

"Never mind about that." Celeste smiled. "I was a teenage girl once myself, you know. Just promise you'll tell me all about your day when we get home."

Nova and Alana exchanged looks. "Sure," they said,

practically in unison.

Since she'd missed their arrival weeks earlier, Nova was not prepared for the cab ride through Paris. Her dad was the only one who seemed unfazed by the chaotic weaving in and out of traffic. Several times, they nearly slammed into other taxis vying for position on the road. Stoplights seemed to have no authority whatsoever to actually stop vehicles. A red light was merely a suggestion. With the exception of Dayton, the whole family was thoroughly rattled by the time they arrived at the airport.

They checked their luggage at the curb and trudged through the long lines at security, finally settling into their seats almost two and a half hours after they'd left the apartment.

"I'm sleeping all the way home," Alana announced.

"Sounds like a plan," agreed Celeste. She put in the complimentary earplugs, leaned her head back, and closed her eyes as the plane took off.

By the time they reached cruising altitude, Celeste and Alana were sound asleep.

Dayton was seated to Nova's left in the center aisle of the plane. He nudged her and whispered, "I've been thinking about Marshall."

"Me too." Nova was exhausted, but her mind was in overdrive.

She needed to talk to him about the tapestry and her plan to go back in. But something important needed to happen first, and these weren't things she could talk to him about on a full airplane thousands of feet in the air. It was better to leave it alone until they were home.

Dayton leaned forward and looked past Nova at Celeste and Alana. He sat back in his seat and asked softly, "Do you want to talk?"

Nova shook her head. "I'm really tired. Can we talk when we get home?"

"Okay, firefly." He was clearly disappointed. He

leaned his head back and stared at the ceiling of the plane.

Nova closed her eyes and pretended to sleep. As they passed over the English Channel her brain finally shut down.

The flight from Paris to London took less than an hour and a half. After a three-and-a-half-hour layover, they boarded the plane for the eight-hour flight to Philadelphia. This time, Dayton had booked first-class tickets. Alana was thrilled with the new accommodations and ran the attendants ragged with her constant requests for drinks and food. Nova was sure the whole flight crew was relieved when she finally passed out over the Atlantic Ocean.

With the time zone change, they landed in Philadelphia at five fifteen in the afternoon, where they easily made their connection. They landed in New Haven shortly before eight. When the airport van dropped them off an hour later, Nova felt like the walking dead. She'd barely slept on any of the flights.

"You girls get some sleep." Celeste hugged them both before dragging herself up the hallway and into her room.

Dayton brought the luggage in, then he disappeared as well.

Nova collapsed on her bed. She'd thought of nothing but seeing Ethan when they were in the air, but now all she felt like doing was crawling into bed.

Alana tiptoed into her room and closed the door. "What's the plan?"

"I don't know. I'm so tired." Nova buried her head in the pillow.

"Not me."

"You slept on the plane… twice."

"Okay. I'll let you sleep then." Alana paused at the door. "We'll talk in the morning, first thing."

Why was she so anxious? As usual, Alana was ready to jump in without fully considering the potential for disaster.

Nova raised her head from the pillow. "Yeah. Tomorrow is better."

She laid her head on the pillow again and closed her eyes. A moment later, she heard Alana close her bedroom door. Nova breathed a sigh of relief and looked at the clock on the bedside table. It read nine o'clock. She closed her eyes and was nearly asleep when the tapping began. It was faint at first. Nova tried to ignore it, assuming it was in her head, a side effect from sleep deprivation. But the tapping continued and grew louder. She pulled the pillow around her head to block out the sound. After a minute or two, it stopped. Convinced she'd imagined it, Nova relaxed and started to drift off… until someone touched her shoulder.

"Wake up, hot girl," Ethan whispered.

She jolted fully awake. "Ethan!"

"Shh!" He clamped his hand over her mouth. "Don't wake the whole house."

She sat up and blinked. "I'm in bed," was all her brain could come up with.

"Really? Thanks for telling me 'cause I never would've figure that out."

Nova couldn't see his face, but she could picture his smug grin. "I was gonna call you tomorrow! What are you doing here?"

"I wanted to see you. I came over, but your house was dark. Normal people don't go to bed this early, you know."

"They do when they just flew thousands of miles on three different planes and can barely remember the last time they slept." She tried to punch his shoulder but couldn't see well enough in the dim room and missed him entirely.

"Nice try, hot girl." He laughed.

She tried again and nailed it this time.

He leaned in close. "I know you're glad to see me."

Nova remembered that she was only wearing a tee shirt, and she grabbed the sheet and pulled it up. "Okay, our house was dark, so you decided to break in?"

"You're funny." He leaned in and kissed her. "And technically, I didn't break in. Your window is unlocked.

That's not very smart, by the way."

"I don't know. It's worked out pretty well so far."

A door closed somewhere down the hall, and they both froze. They heard footsteps, but it sounded like someone was going to the kitchen.

"Was your sister serious that time in the driveway when she said your dad had a gun?" Ethan whispered.

"I don't know." She giggled quietly. "I guess it's possible."

Whoever was walking around was back in the hallway.

"You better go," Nova whispered. "I'll see you tomorrow."

Ethan kissed her again, then hurried to the window and vaulted out. She jumped out of bed and watched him jog across the yard. The footsteps stopped just outside her door. Nova sprinted back to her bed and lay down just as her door opened.

"Why did Ethan leave?"

It was Alana. Nova picked up her pillow and threw it at her sister. Alana dodged it easily.

"Seriously, he's so predictable." Alana grinned and plopped onto Nova's bed. "So, when are you going to tell me your plan?"

Nova pulled the covers over her head. "After I finally get some sleep."

"Fine. But I'm getting you up no later than eight o'clock. I'm setting my alarm."

"Whatever…"

Nova heard the door close but waited a moment before peeking out from under the covers. Her sister was gone.

"Thank God…" She closed her eyes and fell asleep before Alana's door closed down the hall.

Nova heard Aunt Jean calling her name over and

over. She looked around, but there wasn't even a trace of light. Total blackness surrounded her. She groped the air, but there was nothing. She felt panic brewing inside her as she struggled to find anything to hang on to. Then she saw it. Off in the distance was what appeared to be a shimmering silver cloud. She was approaching the tapestry.

Her fear subsided now that she understood where she was. She drifted toward it and heard her aunt calling her again. As she entered the tapestry, she saw her. Aunt Jean looked beautiful, younger and more alive than Nova had ever seen her.

"Aunt Jean!"

"Come on, honey! I want to show you something."

Nova moved quickly toward her, but no matter how hard she tried, she couldn't reach her aunt. "Wait for me!" Aunt Jean retreated deeper into the tapestry, and Nova followed, but still she couldn't catch up. "Aunt Jean, wait!"

Suddenly her aunt stopped. She turned toward Nova and held up her hand, motioning for her to stay where she was. Nova strained to see. Someone small was standing beside Aunt Jean. Someone with sandy hair...

"Marshall!" Nova called.

She heard him laughing, then he turned and disappeared into the tapestry.

CHAPTER 20

Nova woke the next morning with her sister poking her in the arm.

"Wake up!"

Nova groaned. "What time is it?"

"Eight o'clock. Well, more like fifteen after. I didn't jump out of bed the second my alarm went off."

Nova pulled the covers over her head.

"That's not gonna work this time, little sister." Alana poked her again.

"Stop! I'm awake."

"We have to talk. Dad's apparently been up since the crack of dawn. He's on his third cup of coffee, according to Mom."

"Oh my God. I'm dying."

"No, you're not. Just get up. You'll feel better when you're not lying down. It worked for me, anyway."

"You're not normal."

Alana poked her for a third time.

"Stop poking me in the arm! I'm gonna have a bruise."

"Then get up." Alana trotted over to the door and listened. "Dad could show up any minute. We need to talk before he comes in here."

Nova climbed out of bed and pulled on a pair of jeans and a top from her suitcase that was lying open on her floor.

"I need to unpack."

"Later," Alana said. "We need to discuss the plan."

There was no stalling any longer. Nova took a deep breath and let it out. "I want to go see Grandma Kate."

Alana's mouth fell open.

Nova gave her sister a half smile. "Remind me to tell you what Aunt Jean says about catching flies."

Alana ignored her comment. "Why do we need to talk to our grandmother? I thought we were traveling... I mean I thought *you* were going to the tapestry."

"Wait a minute."

Nova stepped into the hall and knocked on the door of Dayton's office. It jerked open almost immediately.

"Good morning, girls." His smile was strained. Nova wondered if he'd slept at all.

Nova's eyes darted up the hallway, but Celeste was nowhere to be seen. "Where's Mom?"

"Running," Dayton answered.

"We need to talk."

He shifted his weight nervously. "All three of us?"

"Yes. Allie needs to be part of things from now on."

He motioned for them to step into the office, then he closed the door behind them. "I don't know how long we have until your mother comes back."

"This won't take long." Nova sat in one of the armchairs that faced his desk and motioned for her sister to take the other one.

Dayton had no choice but to park himself in his leather chair.

When he was seated, Nova continued. "I've given this a lot of thought, and I think we need to go back to Grandma Kate's, like we talked about before our trip to France."

"That's what we said all along. We only waited because... Alana, your heart was set on going. I wanted to give you that."

"I know, Dad." Alana wiped her eyes.

Nova looked between her sister and her dad, wrestling with herself. On the one hand, she wanted to tell her dad everything. But on the other, she was worried that if he knew about the tapestry, he wouldn't want to see his mother again. He'd want to plunge in himself. When she realized that they were both staring at her, she came to a swift decision. She would wait to share that information.

Alana started to say something, but Nova interrupted her. "Aunt Jean said Grandma Kate could help us find the right timeline."

Dayton frowned, obviously choosing his words carefully. "When did you talk to your *dead* aunt about your grandmother?" His eyes darted over to Alana.

Nova felt blood rush to her face. Of course she couldn't have talked to Aunt Jean about traveling. Not recently anyway. She wasn't alive in this timeline. In his mind, she was saying too much in front of Alana. There was only one way out of this awkward situation.

"Okay, fine. I didn't talk to her in *this* timeline. That doesn't matter. Dad, Allie knows everything." Nova almost added, "More than you," but stopped herself just in time.

Dayton pushed his chair back and stood. "What do you mean exactly?" His face had turned red. "Did you tell her about—"

"Marshall?" Alana said softly. "Yeah, she did."

Dayton dropped into his chair again with a thud. His voice sounded weary. "When?"

"I told her in Paris," Nova answered. "Right before we left."

"So, I guess there are no secrets anymore." Dayton sighed.

Nova scooted down into her chair and shot Alana a warning look.

Alana smiled brightly. "Nope. No more secrets. So, when do we leave?"

"You're okay? I mean... you're not upset?" Dayton

sputtered.

"No. My sister is gonna fix this whole mess, aren't you, Nova?" Alana jumped up and headed for the door. "I'm packing. I haven't been to Grandma's since I was little. Do you think she still has that crazy cat?"

And with that, she disappeared up the hall. Nova and Dayton stared at each other.

"What do you think is wrong with her? Have you ever had her tested?" Nova grinned.

Dayton shook his head but smiled in spite of himself. "I think you're both nuts."

"Probably runs in the family. The Grant side anyway."

"So, you girls have decided to go see your grandmother again?"

"Yeah. I think this time will be different," Nova said.

"Why?"

"Trust me, okay?"

"What are you hiding?"

Nova felt her stomach turn over. *Well, Dad, there's this amazing thing called the tapestry. You can use it to travel. As a matter of fact, I've done it myself, and so has Grandma Kate...* Nova swallowed the lump in her throat. "I have a feeling. That's all."

"Fine. We'll drive to Frederick. Maybe we'll stay a little longer this time. Go pack. I'll square it with your mom."

"What if she wants to go too?"

"I doubt she will. I'll tell her we're going somewhere I'm sure she'll pass on. Besides, your school supply list came while we were gone. She wants to get it all this week."

"I like to pick out my own notebooks and things."

Dayton laughed. "You think you'll actually use them?"

"Oh yeah. We won't be here..."

"Bingo."

They heard the screen door slam in the kitchen, and a

moment later, Celeste appeared in the hallway. Her hair was in a ponytail, and her cheeks glowed from her run.

"You look great, Mom," Nova said.

Her mother beamed, clearly pleased by the spontaneous compliment. "Thanks." She pushed a strand of hair from her face. "I'm sure I look a mess." She stepped into her bedroom, still smiling.

Dayton put his arm around her. "That was a nice thing, firefly."

"I meant it. She's beautiful."

"That she is." He smiled.

"Most of our clothes are dirty from the trip," Nova pointed out.

Dayton rolled his eyes. "Okay. Go wash clothes and then pack."

"Shouldn't we say something to Mom first?"

"Maybe we can just sneak out. What's the worst that could happen?"

"She could freak out and ground us."

"Not me." He grinned.

For a moment, he was her old dad—the one who seemed more like a big kid than a grownup.

After breakfast, she and Alana spent the rest of the morning washing clothes. They couldn't pack yet because their mom didn't know they were leaving. Instead, they stacked the clothes they'd need in neat piles on their beds.

A little after noon, Dayton showed up with two pizzas. One was loaded with pepperoni, mushrooms, and green peppers. The other was a Hawaiian pizza with ham and pineapple. That was Nova's favorite. They were all sitting around the kitchen table, happily munching away, when someone knocked on the front door.

Celeste jumped up and disappeared into the hallway. A moment later, they heard her saying, "Come in. We have plenty of pizza. Nova, Ethan's here."

Nova nearly choked on a piece of pineapple.

CHAPTER 21

As soon as he finished bolting down several slices of pizza, Ethan asked if Nova could go back to his house for a couple of hours.

"My parents brought over a load of plants, and they could use some help putting them out." He was using his "impress the parents of your girlfriend" voice.

"If you want to go, you have my blessing." Dayton said cheerfully. "You better grab some work gloves from the garage."

"Sure," was all Nova could manage with everyone looking at her, smug grins on their faces.

After she and Ethan went outside, she rummaged around the garage until she found a pair of worn work gloves that she had absolutely no intention of wearing.

As soon as they were out of earshot, Nova turned to Ethan. "You really volunteered us to plant flowers in your parents' yard?"

"Nah. My parents are still at the nursery picking out what they want. That should take at least a couple of hours." He laughed.

Nova tried to jab him in the side with her elbow, but he easily dodged her. "What did you have in mind then? Cleaning your room?"

"I wasn't thinking of any kind of manual labor." He laughed.

Someone shouted, "Nova Grant, is that you?"

Nova wheeled around. "Yes, Mrs.—uh…" She whispered to Ethan, "Is her last name Wilson or Willard?"

He shrugged.

The old lady was watching them with a stern expression. "You children shouldn't be walking in the road like that. You could be hit by a car."

Ethan caught Nova's eye. "Children?" he mouthed.

"We'll be careful Mrs.—" She stopped herself again. Grabbing Ethan's arm, she steered him onto the grass and kept walking.

Mrs. Wilson or Willard watched them until they were out of sight.

"She keeps turning up," Nova commented.

"Maybe she's not real. Think about it. Has anyone else ever seen her?"

"Funny," she said, goosing him in the side again. This time she got him.

When they turned onto his street, he grabbed her hand and led her around to the back of the house.

"What are we doing?"

"We have to go in the back. I didn't bring a key." Ethan picked up a clay pot from the back porch and flipped it over. The bottom was smooth. "This is where we keep a spare."

Nova leaned in closer. "There's no key there."

"Look." He pushed on the middle of the base, and a compartment popped out. Inside was a key.

"Don't you have your own key?"

"It's in my room somewhere."

"Oh my God. You'll never find it."

"What do you mean?" he asked as he shoved the key in the lock and opened the door.

"Your room is—" Nova caught herself. She'd forgotten that Ethan's mom was still cleaning his room in this timeline. "Never mind."

A golden retriever came bounding into the kitchen and jumped up on Nova, nearly knocking her down. "Hey, Jack." She laughed. "I'm glad to see you too."

"Jack, take it easy, buddy." Ethan grabbed his collar and pulled him off of Nova. "He doesn't act like that with most people. I think he has a crush on you too."

Nova blushed. "He's a sweet dog." She couldn't think of anything else to say.

"Yeah, he has good taste." Ethan smiled and pulled her into a tender kiss.

Nova wondered if he could feel her heart pounding. "Ethan…"

He kissed her again, and she forgot what she'd wanted to say. Suddenly Jack took off toward the front of the house. They heard a car door slam. It sounded like it was coming from the driveway.

"Are you kidding?" Ethan looked out a window in the dining room. "Yep. It's my parents."

A moment later, his mother came through the door, loaded down with a massive fern. "This is for the music room. Ethan, can you take it?" Once she handed the plant off, she saw Nova standing in the hall to the kitchen and smiled warmly. "Nova! How nice to see you."

"Hi, Mrs. Mac." Nova smiled awkwardly, wondering if she knew somehow that they'd been making out in the kitchen.

"I'll send one of these home to your parents. We got in some beauties."

"I don't want to take one of yours."

"Oh, don't worry about that. We have several more at the nursery."

Mrs. Mac took Nova by the hand and led her onto the porch. Ethan had no choice but to follow them outside. Before them were at least three dozen potted flowers and shrubs. Looking at the already abundantly planted yard, Nova couldn't imagine where they all were going.

Ethan read her mind. "Mom, where are you planning to put all these?"

"Here and there. I'll figure it out." She turned to Nova, surveyed her cutoff jeans and tee shirt, and seemed to decide she'd come to work. "Did you bring work gloves?"

"I—uh—no, I didn't," Nova sputtered. "I wish I could help, but I'm going on a trip with my dad and I have to go home and pack."

"Another trip? Didn't you all just get home?" Mrs. Mac asked.

"This one is for my dad's book. It's a research trip. We'll only be gone a couple of days." The truth was, Nova had no idea how long they'd be gone. Maybe forever as far as this timeline was concerned.

Mrs. Mac was clearly disappointed, and so was Ethan. Nova insisted that Ethan stay and help his parents instead of walking her home. She said a hasty goodbye. Halfway back to her house, Ethan caught up with her.

"Tell me about this trip you're taking with your dad." His voice was strained.

Nova really didn't want to do this with him. Not now. He was waiting for an answer though, so she had to say something. "We're going to see my grandmother in Frederick."

"You're going back there? Why?"

Nova sighed. "Can we talk about this later?"

He took her hand. "No. We can't talk about it later. Why are you going back to see her when she wouldn't tell you anything before?"

"Because she *did* tell me something. She told me a lot actually. When I traveled, I saw her in Willow. She told me about some things that might help me get my brother back. I have to talk to her again."

Ethan's face fell, and he let go of her hand. "Oh. I guess you have to go then."

Nova touched his cheek gently. "You knew I was

planning to travel. I can't stop until I have Marshall back too."

"I know, hot girl." He attempted a smile, but it was genuine. "I better get back."

He turned and jogged back toward his house. Nova watched him until he was out of sight, hating that it always ended like this. She trudged home, feeling the weight of it all on her shoulders.

That night at dinner, Dayton brought up the trip. "Babe, I'm thinking of taking the girls with me on a fact-finding outing."

"Oh really? That might be fun. I may go with you."

Nova and Alana looked at each other across the table. If she came along, that would ruin everything. They wouldn't be able to talk to Grandma Kate about the tapestry.

Dayton seemed cool about it. He winked at Nova, then turned his attention to Celeste. "Sure, babe. We're going to hit a few little towns in New Hampshire. I'm scouting locations for a book.

"Oh." Celeste chewed on her lip, something she only did when she was trying to get out of something. "I thought maybe you were going to Boston or New York."

"Nowhere like that. I want to keep the town under ten thousand people. I thought we'd go to local libraries, research the history of each town."

Nova jumped in. "I'm worried about our list of supplies for school. Everything might be picked over by the time we get back."

"I should probably stay home then. I can buy the things you need while you're gone." She looked at Alana. "You're going with them?"

"I'm going." Alana nodded. "Why?"

"It doesn't seem like your type of trip. That's all."

Celeste was right. Normally, there was no way Alana would want to go on a trip like this. It was completely out of character for her.

"I'm broadening my interests," Alana said a little too enthusiastically.

Celeste shrugged. "Well, if you'd rather do that than spend the time shopping for school..."

Alana appeared ready to cave, so Dayton spoke up. "I'm excited that she finally wants to go on one of these jaunts."

Celeste shook her head. "Okay, fine. You all go, and I'll stay here and get the girls ready for school."

Dayton jumped up and gave her a kiss, then proceeded to dance her around the kitchen.

Nova smiled broadly. *Yep. My old dad's still in there.*

CHAPTER 22

The three of them were up the next morning at five thirty in spite of Alana's repeated complaint that no normal person got up that early on purpose. Dayton wanted to miss the morning traffic in town. They loaded the car, ate a quick breakfast, and made it to I-84E heading toward Hartford by six thirty.

Alana shoved the pillow she'd brought under her head. "Why did we bring so much stuff?"

Dayton answered without turning around. "We don't know how long we'll be gone. It could be a couple of days, or we could be back late tonight."

"Whatever. I hope you two have a plan."

She closed her eyes and was sound asleep by six forty-five. Nova envied Alana's ability to shut down no matter what else was going on. She was just like Marshall in that way. Nova stared out the window but didn't really see any of the scenery. She was thinking about her little brother.

"Why don't you try to get some rest too, firefly?"

She looked back at her sister. Alana had claimed the backseat before they left, and Nova could see why. She'd created a sanctuary for herself, complete with a couple of pillows and a cozy blanket.

Dayton tried to see her in the rearview mirror. "Is she wearing a seatbelt?"

Nova looked again. "Believe it or not, she is."

"Okay then." He smiled. "Next stop: Frederick."

Nova was certain she wouldn't be able to sleep, but she leaned her head back and closed her eyes.

***

"Wake up, girls. We're here."

Nova jolted awake. They were just passing the Odd Fellows Hall. She looked in the backseat, but Alana was still sleeping.

"Too bad. She would've loved the whole Odd Fellows story." Nova chuckled. She nudged Alana but got no response. "How does she sleep like that?"

"She's like Marshall." Dayton rubbed his eyes as if they were strained from driving, but Nova wondered if there was another reason.

Alana finally roused just before they turned into Grandma Kate's driveway.

"Are you sure this is right? I don't think it's a driveway," Alana said sleepily.

Nova and her dad looked at each other and laughed.

"What's so funny?" she asked.

"You sound like we did when we came here the first time," Nova answered. "Grandma Kate likes her privacy."

They rounded the curve, and her house came into view.

Alana whistled. "This is more like it."

Kate came out onto the porch and waved as they pulled up. She held the rail as she carefully descended the steps. Nova thought she detected a slight limp. Dayton grabbed the bags from the trunk and followed his daughters up the steps.

"It's wonderful to see you!" Kate threw her arms around each of the girls as soon as she could reach them.

"We're excited to be here." Nova was happy to see her grandmother again, and she was anxious to talk about the tapestry with the only other living relative who had actually been there.

"Thank you for coming and bringing Alana with you." She stepped back and gave her other granddaughter a long look. "My, you look so much like your dad!"

For once, Alana seemed at a loss for words. "Thanks," was all she could manage. This was a whole new side of her, and Nova enjoyed the idea of being the more outgoing sister for once.

Kate held open the door. "Come on in. I have lunch ready."

They followed her inside, but instead of going straight to the kitchen, she took them on a tour of the house—mostly for Alana's benefit since Nova and her dad had been there before. Alana's natural personality emerged from hiding, and she peppered her grandmother with question after question. She knew more about Kate's house in the first ten minutes than Nova had after visiting for hours before.

Under Alana's questions, Kate's reserved shell crumbled, and a different person came out. This Grandma Kate was much more outgoing, and she chattered with Alana as if they were a couple of schoolgirls. She took special delight in showing off Dayton's nautical-themed bedroom and teasing him about his pirate fixation when he was a little boy.

"He actually wanted to pierce one ear and threw a holy fit when I wouldn't let him." Kate laughed.

Alana clapped her hand over her mouth. "Dad, you didn't!"

He gave her a wry smile. "The truth is, I would've rather had the parrot, but she didn't go for that either."

"That's all we needed around here," Kate said, still laughing. "Another mouth that never shut up."

Kate continued cracking jokes about the room, and Alana ate it up. Aunt Jean had described Kate as being full of life, but this was the first time Nova had ever truly seen that side of her grandmother. She wondered if Kate would have stayed like this, outgoing and full of fun, if her first family hadn't been snatched from her.

Dayton stepped into the hall and motioned for Nova to follow him. "I think you and I could leave and it would be hours before the two of them noticed," he whispered, obviously pleased that they were getting along so well.

Nova rubbed her stomach. "I think you're right, but let's eat first."

"Deal."

Alana stuck her head out of the doorway. "Are you talking about food? Because I'm starving."

"Oh goodness! I nearly forgot lunch is ready!" Kate pushed past her and hurried downstairs.

The table was set with a red-and-white checked tablecloth and white dishes. There were daisies in the center of the table. Kate pulled a bowl of chicken salad from the refrigerator, along with a bowl of strawberries and blueberries. She sliced croissants and loaded them with chicken salad, then spooned piping-hot broccoli cheddar soup into the bowls at each place. Once the croissants and fruit were on plates, she motioned for them all to sit.

"This looks delicious, Grandma," Nova said.

"Thank you. I'm glad to have someone else to cook for." She took Nova's hand on one side and Alana's on the other. "Day, would you say grace?"

Dayton swallowed his bite of sandwich whole and proceeded to cough it up while Alana pounded him on the back. Kate sat patiently, waiting for him to recover.

Finally he choked out, "Grace."

Nova kicked him under the table.

"Sorry, Mom. Uh, thank you for this day. And thank you for this food. And thank you for not letting me die just now. Amen."

Kate gave him a stern look. "Out of practice, son?"

He took a long drink of water. "I guess so." He coughed again, and some of the water dribbled down his chin.

Alana cracked up, and the whole table followed.

"Girls, this is what it was like when your dad was growing up. I think he's still in the process."

Nova put her arm around his shoulders. "It's okay, Dad. You don't have to grow up on my account. I like you better this way."

He wiped his chin and dabbed the tablecloth in front of him. "Gee, thanks, honey."

The rest of lunch passed without any more near-death experiences. Mostly, Kate talked about her garden and the pumpkin festival that took place in Frederick every fall.

"Promise me you girls will come back for that. The teenagers have a lot of fun with the pumpkin carving contest. Sometimes they get carried away though. A few of the pumpkins last year had to be disqualified because they were... let's see. How should I phrase this?"

"Racy?" Dayton chimed in. Both girls pretended to be shocked. "Hey, I was a teenage boy once, you know."

When they were finished and the dishes put away, Grandma Kate suggested they sit on the patio in back. Nova loved the gazebo in the garden at Aunt Jean's, but with its brick pavers and ivy-covered trellis overhead, this was just as charming. There were four wrought-iron chairs with yellow cushions and a wooden swing suspended from the beams. Hanging baskets spilled over with purple, yellow, and white flowers.

Once they were seated, Kate said, "It's so nice having you here. I hope you're planning to stay the night."

"We'd love to!" Alana blurted. "We brought overnight bags just in case."

"Well, that settles it." Their grandmother beamed. "Maybe we can go into town later. There's a wonderful ice cream shop on the main road coming in, and I know where to get the best pastries you ever tasted."

"That sounds great." Dayton suddenly looked nervous.

"What is it, Day?" She sat up straight in her chair, her back rigid. "You want to talk about traveling again, don't you?"

Nova jumped in. "We want you to tell us about the tapestry."

"What?" Kate blinked several times, as if she were trying to adjust to bright sunlight after coming from a dark room. "Who told you about that?"

Nova leaned forward and met her grandmother's eyes. "You did."

CHAPTER 23

"Nova, what are you talking about? I never said anything to you about the tapestry!"

"I read about it in Evelyn's journal. And I went there myself. But you were the one who really told me about it."

Kate seemed confused. "I'm sure I didn't."

"It wasn't in this timeline. You were at Willow Hill, and you told me you'd been to the tapestry many times."

"Nova, what…?" Dayton stared at her, his eyes wide. "She doesn't know what you're talking about, and neither do I."

"Grandma knows. She's been there lots of times. She's been with Daniel and watched Danny grow up. She knows all about the tapestry. Don't you, Grandma?"

"How on earth…?" Kate clutched her chest and appeared to be on the verge of swooning.

"Nova, stop this! You're not making any sense."

Alana spoke up. "Let her talk, Dad!"

Nova kept her attention on Kate. "You talked about the tapestry to Aunt Jean and me. Do you remember? In the gazebo in the garden."

Kate's eyes were filled with tears. "Oh my God."

Dayton jumped to his feet. "How did you talk to your grandmother and Aunt Jean at the same time?"

Nova turned to him. "I traveled back to the timeline we were in before. The one you traveled to that day when you went off the bridge in the Mustang."

Her dad was dumbstruck. He opened his mouth but nothing came out.

Nova continued before he had a chance to recover his voice. "I went back to the night I traveled, the night I brought Alana back."

"But your grandmother wasn't—"

"Yes, she was," Nova interrupted.

He dropped into his chair and said quietly, his voice strained, "I don't understand. I thought Aunt Jean told you that you could only go back to the same place if you didn't stay long. That's what you told me. If that's true, traveling back there shouldn't have been possible. We've been here for weeks."

Nova cleared her throat nervously. It was now or never. "I went back through the tapestry."

Kate gasped and knocked over her water glass that was sitting on a small table beside her chair.

"Grandma," Nova said carefully, "I told you I'd been there when we talked at Aunt Jean's. When you told me you'd been there too, you also said that timelines are constantly changing. That's why you were there when I came back. When I was in that timeline before, you'd died years earlier. A car hit you when you were out walking. But when I came back to it, the accident had never happened. You hadn't died after all."

Kate left the porch and came back with a kitchen towel. She wiped up the spill as if she were in a trance, not really noticing what she was doing. No one said anything for a minute or two while she soaked up the water.

Finally Dayton spoke up. "Mom, what is the tapestry?"

When Kate looked up, her eyes glistened with tears. "I never wanted you to know, son. I was trying to protect you. But I should have told you about it. I should have told you everything."

"Okay. Tell me now."

She dropped the towel on the table and sat down again. "Day, there are so many possibilities, so many ways our lives could go. And those possibilities are timelines. They mingle with the timelines we're living in, as well as the ones we travel to or from. Every time a traveler switches to another reality, or someone intersects with yours and alters it in some way, or you face a fork in your road so to speak, it leaves a strand behind. They remain indefinitely, only fading away long afterward." She smiled at Nova. "There's a place where they all are—all the lives you left behind and all the possible futures. My mother called that place the tapestry."

"And you've seen this place?"

"I have," Kate answered.

He looked at Nova. "And you have too?"

Nova nodded.

Dayton frowned. "I don't understand. Where is the tapestry? How do you *use it*?"

Kate sat back in her chair. "I think I'll let Nova explain that."

"I don't know where it is," Nova said truthfully. "But I know how to get there."

"Okay. How do you get there?" Dayton asked, his expression grave.

"At first, you go about it the same way as any other time you travel."

"You forget, I've never traveled the normal way."

Nova *had* forgotten that both times he'd traveled, it had just happened. He had no idea how to control it. "I'm sorry. It's like Aunt Jean said that day in the garden. You sort of put yourself in a meditative state. I usually lie in bed, with my eyes closed, and concentrate on a sound. At Willow Hill, it's the clock."

"The grandfather clock?"

"Yeah. I wasn't even sure it was real until I saw it in Evelyn's room."

Her dad opened his mouth to say something, but apparently thinking better of it, he snapped it shut again, sat back in his chair, and waited.

Nova glanced at her grandmother and Alana. They nodded in unison. It was almost funny.

Nova turned back to her dad. "You feel yourself starting to float. That's where traveling to the tapestry is different. Instead of homing in on a target in time, you wait."

"You don't aim for the tapestry?" he asked.

"No. You don't have a target. But your brain throws visions at you. You have to push them back with your mind. The second you do that, everything stops. You find yourself floating in total blackness. I was so scared the first time. But there's no need to be because that's when you see it."

"The tapestry?" He was hanging on her every word.

Nova had the sudden realization that everything was about to change. Once he knew how to find the tapestry, there would be no way to stop him from trying to do exactly what she planned to do herself. She would have to move quickly. "It looks like a silver cloud. But when you're in it, you see it's made up of countless timelines. The strands are color coded."

"What do you mean?"

"Well, mine are blue. Yours would be a different color."

"Amazing. I wonder what color mine are."

"You'd know them if you saw them. It's hard to explain, but you recognize yours."

"That's pretty cool." He smiled.

Nova smiled too. "If you touch one of your timelines, you can look inside and see yourself. It's surreal in a way. It's not really you that you're watching. It's a possibility. You have to be careful though because it tries to pull you in."

No one spoke for several minutes.

Finally her dad broke the silence. "There's still something that doesn't make sense. If you went back to that timeline, why isn't Marshall here? And why isn't your sister... uh..."

"Dead," Alana blurted out. "The word is *dead*. It's not that hard. Dead, dead, dead. See?"

"Honey, I know you should be... you know."

Alana rolled her eyes. "Dead! Oh my God."

"Stop it, both of you," Nova interjected. "Or you'll have someone else who's dead because my head will explode."

"Don't be dramatic, little sister," Alana huffed.

"Me? You're kidding, right?"

Kate knocked on the table beside her chair. "I'm calling this meeting back to order. No one here is dead. No one's head is going to explode. Let's get back to the point."

"Right," Dayton said, turning back to Kate. "Mom, can we use the tapestry to find Marshall? If it has all of our timelines, he'll be there."

"You're right. He *is* there, in many of your timelines and in Nova's. But the problem is that he isn't in Alana's."

"You don't know that."

"It stands to reason. You and Celeste wanted two children." She gestured toward Nova and Alana. "You have them."

Dayton's face turned red. "So it's hopeless? Is that what you're saying? That seems to be a theme with you."

Nova put her hand on her dad's arm. "It's not her fault, Dad."

"I know. I'm sorry, Mom."

Alana spoke up. "What if I go with Nova?"

Everyone fell silent. Somewhere in the yard, a bird was chirping, but that was the only sound.

"Are any of you gonna say something?" Alana drummed her fingers on the arm of her chair impatiently.

Dayton raised his eyebrows as Nova had seen him do many times. Usually it was when he was amused. But he didn't look amused at all. He looked as if his head was about to pop off. "Go with her where?"

But it was obvious he already knew the answer.

Alana set her jaw. "Into the tapestry. Maybe I'll find him in one of my timelines. Nova said you can only touch your own timelines, so there's no way any of you could look for him in mine. And it figures that if he's in one of mine, Nova will be there too. Problem solved. You'll have all three of us."

Kate shook her head. "If you went together, it probably wouldn't matter."

Nova felt as if all the air had been sucked out of the room. She gripped the arms of her chair. "Grandma, are you saying that Alana and I could be in the tapestry at the same time?"

"Well, yes, I suppose you could—"

"Oh my God!" She jumped up and hugged her grandmother before turning to her sister. "We can go in together! You can look in your strands, and I can look in mine!"

"Didn't you hear me?" Kate asked sternly.

"Yes, but Allie's right. She needs to come with me so she can see inside her timelines. Marshall only has to be in one of them. And maybe if he isn't, there's a way to merge them or something."

Kate frowned. "That's never been done."

"Just because it hasn't been done doesn't mean it can't be done. We won't know 'til we get in there and try. She needs to come in with me."

"What if I came with you instead?" Dayton asked hopefully.

Alana spoke up. "It wouldn't be the same. It has to be me."

"I can't risk losing you both," Dayton said soberly.

Nova's heart rate had returned to normal, and she felt utterly calm. Alana had to go with her. Of that fact she was certain. "Dad, Allie is going with me."

"Okay, then I'll go too."

"No. Allie and I are going. I can't explain it, but I *know* it has to be that way. We'll be all right. I've been there before, and I know how to get out if it we need to."

He lost his resolve and sighed. "Okay, firefly. You win."

***

They spent the afternoon perusing the shops in town, slurping down ice cream cones, and buying chocolate croissants at the tiny bakery. Anyone watching them would have thought they were having a pleasant afternoon, and in a way, they were. But there was also an underlying tension between them. Kate flatly refused to talk any more about the tapestry or anything to do with traveling. It didn't matter. Nova was working on a plan, and she didn't need any more information from her grandmother.

I'm like Evelyn, Nova repeated over and over to herself. *I can figure this out.*

Alana was uncharacteristically subdued, but every time Nova caught her eye, she recognized the same determination in Alana that she felt. They would go in together, and the rest would work out.

They ate dinner at a small café in town called the Iron Skillet. The manager, an older gentleman with gray hair and a wide girth, seemed particularly taken with Kate.

"I haven't seen you in a while, Katie," he said, pulling out her chair. His attention seemed to make her uncomfortable, and she clearly didn't like being called Katie.

"I don't get out much anymore, Robert."

"That's a shame." He gave her a toothy smile. "Who do you have with you?"

"This is my son, Dayton, and his two daughters."

"We're twins." Alana grinned.

"Twins?" He looked back and forth between Alana

and Nova. "I never would've guessed. You don't look alike."

"We're not identical."

"Well, I guess not." He turned his attention back to their grandmother, still flashing his abnormally large, overly white teeth. Nova wondered if they were real. "There's a new movie out this weekend. Would you be interested, Katie?"

She actually flinched when he said her name. "I'll be out of the country."

"That's a shame." He handed out menus and shuffled away dejectedly.

"Mom, you're leaving the country?"

"Of course not," she huffed. "But I have no intention of going out with him."

Alana giggled. "I think I'll use that the next time some annoying guy asks me out."

"Mom, why do you come here?" Dayton asked, looking amused.

"I haven't in a long time, but I thought he'd retired recently, so I thought I wouldn't run into him. I heard he had a heart attack."

"That's awful!" Alana feigned sincerity. "Maybe you should go out with him before he… you know."

"Allie, you're sick." Nova giggled.

The mood at the table lighted considerably.

They ordered their food and talked about inconsequential things as they ate. It was almost nine when they returned to Grandma Kate's house.

"I hope you don't mind, but I'm usually in bed by now. I get up around five," Kate said.

"It's okay, Mom. We're all pretty tired."

Dayton hauled his bag up to his old room in the attic. Nova and Alana were in a guest room next to their grandmother's room on the second floor. There were twin beds with colorful quilts and needlepoint pillows, a night table and a lamp in between them. An ancient TV sat on a large antique dresser facing them.

"Do you want to watch something?" Alana asked sleepily.

"Not really. Besides, it might keep Grandma Kate up."

"I'm not sure that thing works anyway."

"Yeah, it looks pretty old."

"Do you want to talk about—"

"No," Nova interrupted. "I just want to sleep."

"Okay. See you in the morning." Alana rolled over and faced the other direction.

Nova turned out the light, lay in bed, and stared at nothing. She kept going over and over it in her mind. Somehow, she was going to go back to the tapestry with her sister. She'd find Marshall and not come out until they were all together.

***

Dayton steered the Volvo into their driveway in Connecticut at nine thirty the next night. Nova had to drag herself into the house. They were all utterly exhausted after spending most of the day helping Grandma Kate work in her house and yard. After hours of hard labor, Dayton had grabbed a crew working next door and, over Grandma Kate's vigorous objections, paid them to finish the yard work. He'd also made a few phone calls and found someone to paint and do repairs on the house. In spite of her protests, Kate had seemed pleased that he'd taken the initiative to maintain her home.

They'd said their goodbyes after an early dinner, promising to come back in a few weeks even though they all knew that most likely wouldn't happen. They'd be changing timelines long before that.

Nova showered, washed her hair, and blew it dry in record time. She changed into short boxers and a tee shirt and climbed into bed. The clock on her bedside table read ten fifteen. Ethan's parents would still be up. She set the alarm and shoved it under her pillow so it wouldn't wake anyone else when it went off, then she fell straight asleep.

When her alarm went off, she silenced it quickly. The house was quiet. Nova tiptoed into the hallway and listened at Alana's door. There wasn't a sound. She cracked the door open slightly, just to be sure, then quietly closed it again.

She was going to see Ethan, but she had to do something else first—something she hadn't told anyone about, not even her sister. She lay on her bed again and closed her eyes. It didn't take long for her to feel the familiar sense of floating. She would go back far enough to be sure. At least a month before Aunt Jean's funeral. She focused on her target and immediately flew through the tunnel.

And then, she was there. Back at Willow Hill. Standing in the hallway outside Aunt Jean's room. She cautiously knocked on the door and waited. Nothing happened. She tried the knob, and the door swung open. Aunt Jean was standing in the center of the room, putting on a bathrobe. She had flicked on the lamp beside her bed, and when she saw Nova, her mouth dropped open.

"Better close your mouth, Aunt Jean. You might catch a fly."

CHAPTER 24

For once, Aunt Jean seemed to be at a loss for words.

Minutes were ticking by, so Nova said, "I need your help. I'm visiting, so I don't have a lot of time."

"Come in," she said quickly, motioning for Nova to sit in the armchair next to her bed. "You gave me quite a shock, honey. It's after midnight, and to the best of my knowledge, you should be in Connecticut."

"I know. I'm sorry." She tried to collect her thoughts. "I need to ask you something. Grandma Kate said that Alana can go with me into the tapestry. I need to know if *you* think that's a good idea."

Aunt Jean looked at Nova but seemed to be far away. "So the tapestry is real. How did you talk to my sister?"

"Oh my God. This was a mistake." Nova felt herself falling apart. Once again, she'd done something stupid. Of course Aunt Jean wouldn't remember that they'd already talked at length about the tapestry because none of that had happened in this timeline. As far as her aunt knew, Kate was dead.

"I'm guessing by your reaction that we've talked about this before?"

"Yes, with Grandma Kate too."

"I'd love to hear about that, but we have to use the time wisely."

"Yes, we do. I don't want to be stuck here. No

offense."

"None taken, honey." She smiled. "So you and I have talked about the tapestry. And you've also talked to Kate. But you're still having trouble understanding what you should do, right?"

"Right."

"I'm curious about something. How strong is your connection to the timeline you just traveled from?"

Nova concentrated for a moment and easily felt the line back to her bedroom in Connecticut. "It's strong."

Aunt Jean shook her head. "You're just like Mother."

"What do you mean?"

"I think you have longer than you realize before the connection weakens and you have to leave." She sat on the end of her bed. "Step into the hall for a few minutes. Close the door behind you."

"What? Why?"

"Just do it. Trust me. You can keep checking on the connection. If it weakens, let me know. Now go."

Nova did as she was told. She stood outside her aunt's room, constantly checking to be sure the line back to her bedroom was still there. So far, it hadn't faded at all. After a few minutes had passed, she tapped lightly on the door. At first, nothing happened. She couldn't hear a sound from inside Aunt Jean's bedroom.

She was about to knock again when her aunt flung open the door. She seemed excited about something. "Run down to the room at the end of the hall. There's something in there you need."

"You mean Evelyn's room? You want me to get her journal?"

Aunt Jean's mouth flew open again. "How did you know that was my mother's room?"

"You took me there before. Well, not before this. It was—never mind."

"It doesn't matter. Run down there. I'll wait here."

Aunt Jean parked herself in the armchair, clearly dismissing her.

Nova wondered why Aunt Jean was being so weird, but since she could still easily feel the connection, she ran lightly down the hall to the room at the end. When they'd found the journal before, it was taped to the bottom of a drawer. It probably hadn't moved, so she'd look there first.

She turned the knob and opened the door. A light was on beside the bed, and someone was sitting in the rocking chair. She had white hair pulled up in a neat bun, and when she smiled, her whole face lit up. Even from the doorway, Nova could tell that she had the same eyes as her dad.

"I've been looking forward to meeting you, Nova. I'm your great-grandmother."

Nova's feet were rooted to the floor as if they were stuck in concrete. She wondered if she was having some sort of hallucination. This couldn't be Evelyn Grant. She'd died before Nova was born.

"Better come in and get started. We don't have a lot of time."

Nova stumbled over the rug as she tried to get her feet to cooperate. "You're Evelyn?"

"I am indeed." Evelyn smiled warmly. "Now, first things first—can you feel the connection back to where you came from?"

"Yes," Nova said, her voice barely audible.

"Good." She sat down in the rocker again and motioned for Nova to sit on the stool next to her. "My daughter tells me you're a lot like me. If that's true, God help us all." She threw her head back and laughed just like Aunt Jean.

Nova shook herself mentally. She was in the presence of Evelyn Grant, the matriarch of the family, and she was wasting time being starstruck. "Great-Grandma, I need to use the tapestry to get Marshall back. He's my little brother."

Evelyn nodded and waved for Nova to continue.

"I also have a sister, Alana. I don't want to lose her either. But I don't think there's a timeline with both of them. Does that make sense?"

"It makes perfect sense."

"Grandma Kate said I could take Alana with me to the tapestry."

"Of course you can."

"Alana can look in her timelines for one that also has Marshall. But if she can't find one, what can we do?"

"Listen carefully. The tapestry doesn't control you. *You control it.* You have the ability to manipulate it to suit your needs. But it's dangerous, and it can cause irreparable damage if you're reckless with that power. I didn't tell my children about it because, frankly, I thought Bill would blow the whole thing up. He was so impulsive. And I was certain that if my daughters knew about it, they'd eventually tell him. They thought their brother could do no wrong." She shook her head and smiled. "He could have charmed a snake, that one."

"I don't understand. How do I manipulate it? What does that mean?"

"Don't worry. You'll figure it out when you get there. Trust your instincts."

"I need help! Can't you come with me?" Nova pleaded.

"Oh, honey, I wish I could, but I died years ago."

"But you're here!"

"I'm only visiting. Like you." She patted Nova's arm. "Jeannie came to see me a long time ago now. You weren't even born yet. She told me you were here and you needed help. So I came forward. It's not that hard for travelers like you and me. You'll find out that you can do a lot of things you thought were impossible. For some reason, some of us are stronger than others. Not *better.* Just in possession of stronger abilities. But with that extra strength comes more responsibility and more need for self-control. Do you understand?"

Nova nodded.

"All right then, tell me about this boyfriend of yours. My daughter said you've told him about our family." She frowned. "I wish you hadn't. We've never talked about traveling to anyone except other travelers. Your uncle Bill never said a word to Georgia or Michael, and they lived in the same house with him." She shook her head. "Poor Bill was fit to be tied when he realized his only son wasn't a traveler."

"I know I shouldn't have told Ethan. I'm sorry. It kind of happened by accident. I talked to him before I knew about our family. Then once I found out, well…"

Evelyn's expression softened. "What's done is done. No point dwelling on it now. Just remember what I said and be careful."

"Do you know if there are other travelers? Outside of our family, I mean?"

"I suppose it's possible. Why?"

Nova swallowed a lump in her throat. "You probably won't like this, but I hopped back in time at Ethan's. He asked me to."

"Nova Grant! Do I even need to say the words?"

"You mean… stupid? Careless? Irresponsible?"

"Those will do."

"I know. But after I did it, he felt sick, like I did when Dad traveled and changed our timeline. I thought only travelers could feel it when someone changed the timeline."

"What's this boy's name?" Evelyn asked, her interest clearly piqued. "His full name."

"Ethan MacGrady."

Evelyn smiled. "Hand me my Bible from the dresser behind you."

Nova handed it to her, and she opened the front cover. Attached was a folded-up family tree.

"Here we are. I thought so. Uncle Noah's daughter,

Mary Jane, married Ian MacGrady."

"Wha—" Nova's mouth dropped open. "I'm dating a relative?"

Evelyn laughed until her eyes watered. "So far back it doesn't count, honey. They were married in 1855."

Relieved, Nova dropped onto the stool again. "Does that mean he's a traveler too?"

Evelyn shook her head. "Most likely not. As you know, even a few of the Grants aren't travelers."

"I don't know if I'm relieved or disappointed."

"You're probably thinking how nice it would be if he could remember other timelines with you."

"That would be awesome."

"Not to worry, honey. Things usually have a way of working out."

"I hope so, Great-Grandma. I really want to have my whole family *and* Ethan. Do you think that's too much to hope for?"

"No, I don't. Not if you're strong."

"I don't know if I am. I wish you could stay and help me. I think you could do anything. Aunt Jean called you the matriarch of the family."

Evelyn studied her for a moment with a knowing smile. "Actually, I think it's time to pass that title on to someone else." She stood slowly, slightly unsteady. "I hate to cut this short. I've so enjoyed getting to know my great-granddaughter a little." Evelyn frowned slightly. "But I'm not as strong as I used to be. My connection is fading. I have to leave."

Nova closed her eyes and concentrated. She could still feel hers, but it wasn't as strong. When she opened her eyes again, Evelyn was looking at her with a peaceful expression.

"I wish we had more time," Evelyn said softly.

"Me too, Great-Grandma." Nova's eyes filled with tears. "I wish I could've known you."

"I was a cantankerous old broad, believe me." She chuckled. "Now give me a hug before I go."

Nova wrapped her arms around her great-grandmother's delicate frame. "Thanks for coming to see me."

"It was my very great pleasure. Now run along. I have to go back, and I'm not accustomed to traveling in front of anyone."

Nova wiped her eyes. "Will I ever see you again?"

Evelyn smiled wistfully. "There are endless possibilities, honey. You just might."

Nova left the room without looking back. She hesitated at Aunt Jean's door, then proceeded down the hall to the room she'd claimed as her own since her first time at Willow Hill. She opened the door and stepped inside. Even though none of her things were there, it still felt like her space, her own personal sanctuary.

She opened the window and climbed onto the four-poster. The familiar sounds from the garden drifted in. She lay there a minute or two, enjoying being back. She could still feel the connection, but it was fading quickly. It was time to leave.

Everything was about to change. But first she had to do one more thing. She closed her eyes and let the tether pull her back to her room in Connecticut.

CHAPTER 25

Nova lay on her bed at home, waiting for her heart rate to slow down. Eager to get going, she took a couple of deep breaths. That seemed to help.

She'd tucked a pair of shorts and a shirt under her covers earlier. She pulled them on and slipped her feet into a pair of sneakers before arranging her pillows under the covers in a way that made it look as if she was there sleeping. At least she hoped so. It wouldn't do for either of her parents to come in and find her missing.

She tiptoed to the open window and climbed through, dropping lightly to the ground. Ethan would be in bed. She couldn't call him this time of night, so she'd have to wake him some other way. Nova picked up a handful of pebbles from the road and stuck them in the pocket of her shorts.

She looked back at her house and thought of her family sleeping inside, unaware that sometime that night, everything was going to change. Part of her wanted to go back and crawl into her bed again. She stood perfectly still, watching her house and thinking about the tapestry. *It has to work this time.*

She turned away and walked to Ethan's house. It was nearly two o'clock in the morning. Every house she passed was dark, the people inside sleeping peacefully. A wave of envy washed over her. It would be so much easier to be like everyone else—to not have the burden of fixing things that went wrong. But if that were the case, if she were like every other person who couldn't travel, her dad would still be dead... and so would Alana. She sighed. This life was hard, but it was still better than the alternative.

She stood in the driveway of Ethan's house for several minutes, wondering exactly what she was going to say to him. At that moment, she had no idea. The house was pitch dark, which made total sense at two o'clock in the morning. She walked around to the back and looked up at his window. He was probably sound asleep.

Nova pulled out one of the pebbles and tossed it at the window, missing it by a good two feet. She threw another one, but it ended up in the gutter on the edge of the roof. On the third try, the stone hit one of the window panes squarely in the middle and produced a surprisingly loud *clink*. She crouched and waited, half expecting Ethan's dad to come around the corner to see who was throwing rocks at their house. Two or three minutes passed and no Mr. MacGrady. Nova heaved a sigh of relief and retrieved another stone from her pocket. She was about to toss it when the window shot open and a shirtless Ethan leaned out. Nova fell backward and almost rolled down the hill.

"What's up, hot girl?" He grinned.

She jumped up and brushed off her shorts, trying not to pay attention to the fact that as far as she could tell, he could be naked. "I wanted to... I just came over to see you."

"Come to the back porch. I'll let you in."

Nova stepped onto the porch, her heart pounding. As she waited anxiously for him to open the door, she thought about what she wanted to say to him—all of which flew out of her head the moment she saw him. He was wearing sweatpants, but still no shirt. Nova felt as if she'd swallowed a jar of butterflies.

He held the door for her and whispered, "My mom's an insanely light sleeper, so be really quiet 'til we get to my room."

Nova nodded and followed him through the kitchen and down the hall.

Once they were behind closed doors, Ethan wheeled around to face her. "What's going on?"

"Nothing." Nova tried to collect her thoughts, but it was hard with him standing there half-naked. "Can you put on a shirt?" She felt her face go bright red.

"Sure." He pulled a tee shirt out of a pile of clothes on the floor.

Under normal circumstances, she wouldn't have been able to resist teasing him about the mess. But she couldn't shake the feeling that this might be the last time she saw him for a long time, if ever again.

"Sorry my room's so messy. My mom went ballistic yesterday and said it was up to me if I wanted to live in a pig sty."

"It's fine."

Ethan picked up on her mood and was uncharacteristically serious. "Are you okay?"

Nova fought off the overwhelming urge to break down and sob. What if her plan backfired and she lost everyone, including Ethan? What if this time, her whole life changed in ways that were impossible to fix? Why did she think she could do something no other traveler had done?

"Come here," Ethan said softly, pulling her to him.

She laid her head on his chest and cried. "I'm sorry."

"For what?"

"All of it. Making you deal with everything. Not remembering…"

Ethan slipped his hand up her back and pulled her even closer, then cupped her chin and kissed her tenderly. "It doesn't matter."

She let herself be drawn in before replying. "It matters to me. It's not fair. I want to remember meeting you in the fifth grade. I want to remember getting the bracelet from you and going to your house—every minute we spent together in the other lives. I'm tired of starting over, trying to keep up with a history I won't ever remember."

"I'm sorry," he said softly.

"And that's not all. There are things I'll remember that you never will. You don't know about the caretaker's house, or the cemetery, or the gazebo at midnight."

"What are you talking about?"

She pulled away from him. "I have to go."

"Nova?" He spoke so softly she wasn't sure he'd actually called her by her name. He pulled her close again. "Don't go. Stay with me."

After a few minutes, she stepped back again. "I'm so sorry."

He took her hand. "Wait."

"Ethan, I have to go. I'm sorry I came over. I just wanted to tell you how much I love you."

He took her face and kissed her until she tasted tears. She wasn't sure if they were hers or his.

She backed away and fled down the hall, through the kitchen, and out the back door, half expecting him to run after her. But there were no footsteps behind her. She heard the door close loudly, but she didn't care. It didn't matter if she woke the whole neighborhood. She let herself sob in earnest all the way home. If someone had looked out and seen her running by, they might have run after her or even called the police over the sobbing teenager running by at two o'clock in the morning. She didn't care. Nothing mattered anymore. She was leaving this timeline forever. It would eventually fade inside the tapestry until it was gone. She let the tears pour until there were no more.

She crawled in through her window and lay on her bed, staring at the ceiling that used to have a spider carcass. She couldn't cry anymore. She felt numb.

Alana burst into her room. "I thought you'd never get home. How'd it go with Ethan?"

Nova turned her face away.

"Wow. That well, huh?"

Nova looked back at her sister. "I don't want to talk about it."

"Fine with me. So… when are we gonna—"

"Now."

"Are you sure? Do you want some time?"

"No. I'm ready. We need to leave now."

Alana climbed onto Nova's bed and sat cross-legged. "Okay, little sister. First, tell me more about the tapestry. I want to be prepared."

Nova didn't feel like going over it all again, and she didn't want to share her experience with their great-grandmother. That visit had been something between the two of them. Evelyn had said that Nova was like her—stronger than other travelers. What would be the point in telling Alana about that?

"Nova!" Alana said impatiently.

"I've told you everything I know."

"I was wondering though… how do you feel when you're there? I mean, are you like a spirit floating around, or is it just a place in your mind?"

Nova was taken aback. That was actually an excellent question. She sat up and thought for a moment. When she had visited the tapestry, for the most part she'd felt like herself. She'd touched the timelines and felt the sensation in her hand. She'd even heard her own voice. "It's not in your mind… and you're not a spirit."

Alana cocked her head. "So you really are physically there." It wasn't a question.

"Yeah. You're there."

Alana chewed her lip nervously. "How do we get there? I mean, I know the process. But how do we get there *together*?"

Nova frowned. "We travel at the same time and hope we find each other once we're inside."

For the first time, Alana seemed really nervous. It

was a little unsettling. Alana was the brave one who jumped first and thought about it later. Obviously her sister expected Nova to know everything, but in reality, she had no idea how any of their plan was going to work.

"Okay. But once we're actually in the tapestry, let's give it a certain amount of time. Then if we don't find each other, we come back. Agreed?"

Nova shook her head. "There's no way to tell time in there."

Alana thought about that for a minute. "Then I guess we just head back when it seems like we've been there long enough. Deal?"

Nova nodded and took Alana's hand. "We'll do this together, no matter what. Okay, Allie?"

"Okay, little sister. No matter what."

Nova closed her eyes and took a deep breath, slowly and deliberately. She instinctively knew that her sister was doing to the same. The sensation of floating came quickly. It was becoming so easy to travel. She was stronger each time.

She held back a little before going into the tunnel in case Alana wasn't there yet. She heard her sister beside her, breathing steadily, but couldn't tell how far along she was. After a few minutes, the pull became too strong to resist, and Nova let herself slip into the tunnel. Her brain bombarded her with images while she felt her body being tossed around. It was easier to fight the current and push away the visions than it had been the first time she'd found the tapestry. She was worried about Alana though and prayed that she was strong enough to fight it.

Suddenly, Nova was in the pitch-black void, but this time, she felt no fear at all. She knew she was moving even though she could see nothing. Any moment now, the silvery web of the tapestry would appear. She strained to see ahead, hoping desperately that her sister had also made it through. There was no turning back either way.

We'll do this together, Nova repeated silently, over

and over.

Minutes passed as she floated, waiting. And then, there it was, off in the distance. The shimmering silver cloud.

CHAPTER 26

Nova entered the tapestry and felt the familiar sense of awe. If anything, it was more magnificent, with glittering strands shooting off in every direction. Most had the bluish glow that identified them as hers. Other strands of different hues intersected hers or joined them briefly before disconnecting and moving off on a separate path. Nova looked around for Alana but couldn't see her.

"Allie!" Her voice sounded strange, as if she was in a deep well and calling for help.

She listened intently, but the only sound was a slight crackling from the timelines around her. She'd never noticed it before. Maybe she was becoming more aware with each visit. Nova moved slowly into the labyrinth of timelines, but she still couldn't see her sister, and calling for her produced no results. Maybe Alana wasn't there yet. Maybe she was still at home, sitting cross-legged on the bed, trying to see the tapestry.

She called again, "Allie! Are you here?"

Nothing.

Aunt Jean's words played in her head. "Unless God made you the center of the universe, the tapestry you were in was one that was made up of your timelines."

Nova looked at all the timelines that were glowing blue. They were hers. She was in her own tapestry, so it would stand to reason that the other travelers had their own tapestries as well. Other strands intersected with hers. Her sister's strands were glowing lavender. She couldn't say how she knew they were Alana's, but she was sure they were. Nova felt like screaming. Had she sent her sister into her own tapestry all alone?

"Allie," she called out again. But there was no response.

Nova moved deeper and deeper into the tapestry, searching for more of her sister's strands—timelines that glowed a brighter lavender. She called repeatedly for her as she drifted along, until suddenly Alana answered. She sounded far away.

"Nova!"

Nova jerked around and felt a wave of utter relief. Alana was no more than thirty feet from her.

"This place is incredible!" her sister gushed. "I can't believe it's real!"

Nova reached out to her. "We have to stay together!"

Alana came closer. "Now what, little sister?"

"You have to look for Marshall in your timelines."

"I don't even know what he looks like."

"He looks like the picture I showed you in the office. You thought he was one of Dad's book people."

Alana cocked her head. "The kid who looked like me?"

"Yeah. The kid who looked like you."

"Okay, got it." She drifted upward and touched one of her strands. Immediately, an aura surrounded her, almost as if she were part of the lifeline. "Oh my God." She hovered there for a moment, then slowly began to disappear.

"Allie!" Nova shouted.

Alana jerked back from the timeline. "Wow. I almost went inside." She seemed shaken up.

"You have to be careful." Nova grabbed her arm. "You can't let it pull you in."

"I'll be more careful next time," Alana said

breathlessly. "I don't know how this is gonna work. I was at school. Even if he's in there, I won't necessarily look in the right spot."

"Once you get control, you can go back and forth in that life. Try again."

Alana approached another lavender strand and reached out hesitantly. Once again, she was surrounded by an aura, but this time, her image didn't fade. She slowly moved along the thread that represented that one possible life. Nova knew from experience that even though she appeared to be moving slowly, she was actually rocketing through that life. After a few minutes, Alana pulled away.

"Did you see him?" Nova asked hopefully.

Alana shook her head. She continued looking into her timelines, one after another, always with the same results.

"He's not in mine," she finally said sadly.

"Keep looking," Nova pleaded.

"Face it, little sister. He won't be in any of mine."

"You don't know that!" Nova felt a wave of panic overtake her. This wasn't working, and deep down, she knew Alana was right.

"Nova, look around. I don't have that many timelines. Maybe I'm not supposed to live. Maybe that was the plan all along."

"No! I don't believe that!" Nova practically screamed.

Alana shook her head. "If it's me or Marshall, I think he wins. It's okay, little sister. I don't want to be the reason––"

"Stop it! You're *both* supposed to live! I know it. Just give me a minute." Nova closed her eyes, desperately groping for any shred of memory, anything her grandmother had said about the tapestry. There was something she wasn't remembering—something that could change everything. What was it?

Alana said sadly, "All these strands are so dim…"

"It doesn't matter! Once you connect with one, it'll come back. But I think we need to go back to where we were. There were lots more timelines—yours and mine."

"What about Marshall?"

"We'll find one with him too."

Nova wished she felt more sure. Truthfully, she had the worst feeling imaginable—that she might actually lose her sister again. And this time, it would be forever.

"You look in yours for a while," Alana said. "I'm tired."

Nova moved back to the section she'd passed through earlier. Her most brilliantly lit threads were there. She touched one. She was sitting on the bridge, her feet dangling over the edge. Nova knew instinctively that her dad was dead in this one. She recognized this sad version of herself.

She moved on to the next one, and the next, and the next, until she lost count of how many she had seen. One thing was certain—Marshall was alive in most of them, and Alana wasn't. In spite of that fact, Nova had the feeling that she was missing something. If she could only remember.

"What do you see, little sister?" Alana asked hopefully.

"I'm still looking."

"What about the last one?"

"It's not one we can use. You were…"

"Dead."

"Yeah." There was another blue strand just ahead. "I'll check this one. Sooner or later…"

"Enough of this!" Alana blurted. She reached for the timeline before Nova could stop her. There a loud crackle, then a blast threw Alana back violently.

"Allie!" Nova screamed, moving toward her unconscious sister. It appeared that she wasn't breathing. "No, no, no! Don't die in here!"

Alana's eyes fluttered, then opened. She seemed far away. After a few minutes, she came around. "What h-happened?"

"You tried to get into one of my timelines. You can't do that! You can't touch any timelines that aren't yours!"

"Then it's hopeless." Alana wept. "Just leave me…"

"Wait! I know there's a way."

"There isn't a way!" Alana sobbed. "There aren't any timelines that have all of us. It's not like we can make one."

Nova gasped. That was it! The thing she'd forgotten. The thing Grandma Kate had said in the garden. "Oh my God, Allie! I know what to do."

She grabbed Alana's hand and pulled her back through the web of timelines.

"What are we doing?" Alana's voice was weak.

"Hold on. I need to find the right one. I want to be sure."

Nova let go of her sister and continued to look into timeline after timeline. Every time she touched one, it glowed with more intensity. She still hadn't found the one she was looking for, so she kept moving.

Alana had stopped looking for any of hers. It was just as well, because Nova knew what she had to do.

She reached out again and felt her heart pound. This was the one. She saw herself in the office with Ethan, looking through a drawer just before her parents arrived home from Marshall's school. She moved a little farther back in that timeline and saw Dr. Cheerful grilling her at the hospital. She continued to move back in the timeline—Ethan leading her through the woods… Delilah snubbing her on the bus… the plate of waffles on the table that morning. She came to an unfamiliar scene, one she hadn't been able to remember because she hadn't lived it before. She was seated at a lunch table with Ethan. He rubbed the corner of her mouth with his thumb. "You're supposed to eat the ice cream sandwich, not rub it on your face." He laughed.

"Allie, this is the one!" she called.

There was no answer.

She looked around frantically and spotted her sister. She was drifting away. "No! Allie, wait!"

Alana stopped where she was and stayed there, motionless. Nova kept moving closer to Alana in the tapestry, but farther and farther back in the timeline. She saw herself at the hospital, her hand wrapped in gauze. Her mom was beside her, explaining to the young doctor that the bus driver had closed the door on her daughter's hand. The doctor removed the bull dog bracelet from her wrist and laid it on the bed beside her, but it fell on the floor. A moment later, a nurse came in and accidentally kicked it into the hall, where a little girl with a tear-stained face and arm in a cast picked it up. Her parents were following her in the hall, and they looked into Nova's room.

"Is this yours?" the mother asked.

"She can keep it," Nova responded.

Nova pulled away from the timeline and looked for Alana. She seemed to be drifting farther and farther away.

"Allie! You have to come toward me!"

Her sister didn't respond. She had turned back and was moving deeper into the tapestry.

"No, wait!" Nova called.

Nova looked back at the timeline and, without reaching out, followed it along as far as she could see. She could move in Alana's direction only so far before she'd have to leave the timeline behind and possibly lose it. "Allie! Stop there! I need to tell you something."

Alana looked back. She seemed uncertain whether to wait or continue on. "Just leave me! If I'm gone, Marshall can have a life. You have so many lives that include him and not me. And I can stay here."

Nova couldn't move any closer to her sister without losing the strand. She could barely reach it now. "I know a way we can all be together. Please trust me."

"You can't make it happen just because you want to."

"Yes, I can. We can make a whole new timeline."

Alana still seemed uncertain, but she stopped moving away. "That's not possible." But there was hope in her voice. She moved a little closer.

"You're right. It shouldn't be possible. But then none of this should. Look around you. Should *this place* be possible?"

"What are you going to do?"

"We're going into this timeline together."

Alana moved closer still. Nova could almost touch her. "I can't touch your strands. Only mine."

"You won't. Trust me."

Alana cried, "What if it doesn't work?"

Nova reached out to her. "I know it will. Take my hand."

Alana hesitated, then moved closer and reached out until their fingers met. Nova gripped her sister's hand and turned back to the timeline. It was just out of reach.

"We have to move closer…" Nova strained to touch it. She looked back at her sister pleadingly. "You're the brave one. Help me."

Some of the spark returned to Alana's eyes. "I'm with you, little sister."

She moved in closer, and Nova touched the timeline. She didn't immediately see herself in that life, as had happened before. Instead, her whole body quivered as flashes of dazzling light swirled around them. There seemed to be every color of the rainbow—their own personal aurora borealis. Nova hung on to Alana's hand even as it radiated an unnatural heat, as if her body temperature had jumped ten degrees.

Nova looked back at Alana again. An aura of brilliant light surrounded her. Nova was awestruck. "Can you see that?"

Mesmerized by the lights, Alana didn't answer at first. But then she reached out with her other hand and touched Nova's face. "Where's your light coming from?"

Careful not to break the connection, Nova turned back to the timeline. She tried to throw herself in... to no avail. Maybe she couldn't enter with her sister after all! *No! This has to work!* Alana's hand seared hers. The pain was almost unbearable, but still Nova held on.

"What's happening?" Alana shouted.

The strand seemed to be on fire as Nova held on. "Please let me in!"

Alana pointed upward with her other hand, her voice fearful. "What's that?"

Nova jerked around and saw it. Another thread was descending rapidly toward them. It glowed with an almost blinding intensity, more brilliant that any of the others. They watched it weave in and out of the other timelines until it connected with Nova's in a brilliant flash of electricity that jerked her violently into that reality.

Nova slammed into a wood floor, knocking the air out of her lungs. She gasped and tried to inhale, but only managed a tiny breath before falling into a coughing fit. When she could finally suck in a lungful of air, a wave of nausea followed. She rolled onto her back, took a deep breath, and let it out slowly.

"Allie, are you here?" Nova choked out, her voice barely audible.

No reply.

"Allie!" she called again, more loudly this time.

"I'm here." Alana's voice sounded different—*smaller*.

Relief washed over Nova. They had made it together to... wherever they were.

She rolled onto her stomach and pushed up on her hands and knees as another rush of nausea hit her. "Why am I sick? I'm not supposed to feel it if I'm the one who traveled."

"I'm sick too," came Alana's faint reply. "I think I'm gonna throw up... and my head hurts."

Nova grabbed the bed beside her and pulled herself

onto it. "I think we're home."

The room had that waning twilight look—not exactly pitch black, but dim and shadowy. She saw the streetlight filtering through the tree outside her window. There was a bed beside hers, and she could make out Alana's form. She was sitting up.

"I guess we share a room." Nova's voice sounded a little raspy, not like herself. She tried to clear her throat and shake the fog from her brain.

They should be up, exploring their new surroundings and figuring things out, but neither of them moved. Every muscle in Nova's body ached. She couldn't remember ever feeling this exhausted.

"Nova?" Alana's voice still sounded funny.

"What?"

"I feel kind of… *weird.* Do you?"

Weird was as good a word as any to describe how she felt. "Yeah, I definitely feel weird."

The light on the nightstand between their beds flicked on. Alana sat across from her, frozen, her hand still on the light switch and her mouth hanging open in shock. Nova stared at her, her mind refusing to accept what her eyes were seeing. Alana wasn't the sixteen-year-old twin who had taken her hand in the tapestry. This Alana was a child. She couldn't be much older than Marshall.

"Why are you so young?" Alana asked frantically. "We're supposed to be the same age! We're twins!"

Nova said nothing. She continued to stare, her eyes as big as silver dollars.

"Nova! I don't understand. Why aren't you my age?"

Nova finally answered, her voice barely audible. "I think I am."

Someone cracked open the bedroom door.

"You girls keep it down," Celeste whispered. "If you wake Marshall, we'll never get him back to sleep."

Nova spoke up. "Where's Dad?"

"Sleeping, like you should be. Now, lights out, girls." She smiled as she closed the door softly.

Alana jumped onto Nova's bed and hugged her hard. "We did it, little sister!"

Nova wiped her eyes. "Yeah… but how old do you think we are?"

"I don't know. Ten maybe?" Alana whispered, "You want to hear something really strange?"

"Stranger than this?"

"Kind of. I'm okay with it."

"What?"

"I'm okay not being sixteen."

"You are?" Nova thought about it. Now she'd have years of memories with her sister that she'd missed the first time she'd been in this life. And her little brother was back. It was everything she'd hoped and prayed for. Her whole family was here. She smiled. "I'm okay too."

"We'll be better at everything! School, driver's ed, going on dates. The whole thing."

Nova thought of Ethan and blushed. "After a while, we probably won't remember what it felt like—being a teenager."

"I won't forget. You want to know something else cool?"

"Sure. Why not?" Nova grinned.

Alana flashed a mischievous smile. "I'm gonna be a great kisser."

"Oh my gosh." Nova giggled.

***

Nova leaned her head against the window as the bus turned onto Riverbank in the opposite direction of the bridge. The kids around them were making a racket, but the bus driver seemed oblivious. Someone across the aisle threw a banana peel and hit a boy two rows up in the back of the head. He grabbed it from the floor and hurled it back at no one in particular while the kids around them squealed.

Alana squeezed her hand. "Be brave, little sister. It's gonna be okay."

"I hope so," Nova answered quietly.

Alana whispered in her ear, "You know, someday we're gonna have to tell Dad what we did."

"I know." Nova looked out the window again. In a few years, they'd be riding the bus to the high school. They'd cross the bridge every day. She wondered if she'd even remember the accident by that time. She caught her reflection in the window and stared for a moment before looking back at her sister. "I don't feel like I did before. Do you?"

"You mean like a teenager?" Alana asked.

Nova nodded.

"No, I guess I don't."

They filed off the bus and through the doors of Samuel Clemens Elementary School. Nova watched Alana walk down the hall toward her fifth-grade classroom. Two girls joined her, laughing and talking a mile a minute. One of the girls tossed her hair over her shoulder just like the teenage version of her had done at the party. Chelsea or maybe Lauren. Nova had never figured out which was which. She smiled as the girls disappeared around the corner with Alana in tow. Apparently her sister was destined to be popular in any timeline.

Nova looked at the class list in her hand. Her teacher was Mrs. Montcastle. She continued down the hall until she saw her name on the door. Nova took a deep breath and stepped into her classroom. Mrs. Montcastle was standing at the front of the room, checking off names and assigning desks on a first-come-first-serve system. The first ones in the room were stuck with the front row, which was now populated by some very unhappy students. Nova was relieved to find herself in the second row and next to the windows.

She plopped down in the chair and shoved the contents of her book bag into her desk. Someone took the desk beside her, but she didn't look up. Suddenly shy, she took as long as she could to arrange her supplies. She'd never had Alana's confidence when it came to dealing with their peers and hated those first few minutes meeting someone new. She pretended to be engrossed in organizing her desk for as long as she could. Any longer and everyone would think she was some kind of neat freak.

Nova took a deep breath and pushed her empty book bag under her seat. When she cautiously glanced at the person sitting beside her, her throat went dry and she felt her heart skip a beat.

He studied her with his dark-blue eyes for a split second, then he grinned, exposing a dimple in his right cheek. "Hi. I'm Ethan."

THE END

EPILOGUE

Nova sat on the porch swing, watching him navigate the branches of the giant oak tree that towered over the house. The ladder only reached so far, so he had decided to climb the rest of the way. The rope was wrapped around his arm several times and attached to a tire dangling far below. Every time he moved, the tire banged against the ladder, making it sway back and forth. Nova held her breath as the tire bounced against the trunk of the tree, then smacked into the ladder again. This time it nearly fell. She contemplated going back inside, but the image of him plunging twenty feet to the ground kept her from moving. She imagined his lifeless body sprawled out under the tree and a chill ran up her spine. She pulled her cell phone out of her pocket, just in case.

Nova wrapped her sweater more tightly around her shoulders. The days were getting cooler. Some of the leaves had already changed into the brilliant yellows, oranges, and reds of fall. The squirrels were turning out in droves to collect acorns. It was her favorite time of year, magical and full of color.

Nova closed her eyes and let the motion of the swing relax her until the relative peace was disrupted. Birds who had taken up residence in the massive oak were voicing their displeasure over the unwelcome visitor carrying a rope. The occasional peep had turned into frantic chirping as they loudly expressed their concern over the fact that a human was encroaching on their territory. She opened her eyes just in time to see him nearly fall as one of them swooped down, almost landing on his head.

"I think that's high enough," Nova called.

"Almost there," he answered as he waved away another feathered kamikaze.

After several attempts to chase him off, the birds reluctantly returned to the higher branches and talked among themselves, most likely planning their next move. Nova let her head rest against the slats of the swing as she watched him climb even higher into the tree. He noticed her watching and gave her a thumbs-up. She found some small comfort in the fact that pretty soon he'd run out of limbs that could accommodate a tire swing and he'd have to come down.

She anxiously watched his progress as the familiar sound of rushing water drifted up the hill. It was ironic that she'd chosen to live in a house overlooking the river that had long ago caused her so much pain. But the memory of that time had retreated into the most remote region of her brain, the place where old dreams were stored and barely remembered. Now the river was more like an old friend, comforting and steadfast.

A yellow school bus turned onto the road below and sputtered to a stop. The doors sprung open, and two children got off, a boy and a smaller girl. Both of them waved as they started up the hill. Nova waved back, smiling. A few minutes later, the screen door slammed as the little girl joined Nova on the porch.

The little girl was eating a cookie and grinning. "Day gave me his cookie from lunch." Her golden-blond curls cascaded over her shoulders and halfway down her back.

"Did he now?" Nova tried to fake a stern face, but the little girl giggled. "I guess it's okay since your brother gave it to you."

"That's what I thought too." She seemed very proud of herself for making the decision.

Another bus approached, and the little girl leaned on the rail, watching for it to stop.

"That's not Daniel's bus, Evie. Middle schoolers don't get out this early." Nova pulled her onto the porch swing, and the little girl cuddled against her.

"Push harder," she demanded.

Nova obliged, pushing off amid peals of laughter until the swing was nearly horizontal to the porch floor.

"Hey, you two! Be careful!"

"You're the one in the tree," Nova called back.

"Don't worry, hot girl. I've got this." He grinned from his perch.

Evie looked up with large hazel eyes and frowned. "Is Daddy gonna fall?"

"No, sweet girl. He's not going to fall." Nova hoped that was true. She watched Ethan swing the rope over a massive branch at least twenty-five feet from the ground.

"Is Aunt Allie coming today?" Evie asked, already thinking of something else.

"Yes. Aunt Allie, Uncle Luke, and the twins."

Evie wrinkled her nose. "Max is okay I guess, but Charlie talks too much."

Nova chuckled. "More than you?"

Evie nodded vigorously. "Lots more."

Nova laughed.

"Who's sleeping in my room?" Evie asked.

"Aunt Jean."

Evie sat up, obviously excited. "Oh, I don't mind Aunt Jean taking my room! She's my favorite!"

"I know she is." Nova gave her daughter a hug. "Grandma Kate and Grandpa Dan are coming too."

"Where are they gonna sleep?"

"They're staying down the road at your grandparents' house."

"Papa Day said he's writing a story about me. He's putting in pictures and everything. I'm gonna show everybody at school."

"You'll be famous. Your grandfather's a great writer, you know."

"I know. But Grammy says he's a big kid."

Nova whispered in her ear, "Well, just between you and me, I think she's always secretly liked him that way."

"Is Uncle Marshall bringing Elizabeth?"

Nova nodded, amused by how quickly her little daughter's brain hopped from one thought to the next. "Of course. In a few days, she'll be your aunt Elizabeth. You're in the wedding."

"I carry the flowers."

"That's right."

Evie cuddled into her mom again and said nothing for a few minutes. Suddenly, she sat up and pointed. "Look how high Daddy is in the tree. Are you sure he won't fall?"

"He won't fall," Nova assured her even though she was worried about the same thing.

"If he does, will you fix it? Like last time?"

Nova threw her head back and laughed. "Yes, Evie. Just like last time."

Willow, North Carolina

Willow was inspired by a real town in North Carolina. Just like in the story, train tracks split the main street right down the middle. I've stood on the bridge that arches over the tracks and watched a train speed by underneath. I've eaten a chicken salad sandwich with homemade chips in a café across the street, and across the tracks, from the feed store. I've browsed through the antique shops along the main drag and bought hand blown ornaments in the Christmas shop. It's a picturesque, historic town.

Willow Hill was inspired by a horse farm about twenty minutes from the town. With rolling pastures, a large state-of-the-art stable, and a tree-lined drive, it's a beautiful sight. In the spring, you might see mares grazing peacefully in the pasture by the road, their foals frolicking nearby. I actually got out of my car to watch them.

The magnificent brick house with a two-story porch sits so far back from the road that the woman who lives there rides a three-wheeled ATV to pick up the mail. She's approximately sixty years old, with wheat-colored hair just beginning to gray. As I passed, she waved, as people in the country often do. I like to think of her as Aunt Jean.

Frederick, New Hampshire

Frederick was inspired by a real town in New Hampshire. There really is an Odd Fellows Hall on the main street through town. After you pass the bandstand, you can't miss it.

There is also a store called Willow, and an ice cream shop with any flavor you can think of. Clapboard houses, most of them built many years ago, festooned with flowers in window boxes line the streets. Blooming shrubs and massive trees abound.

In October, the whole town comes out for the Halloween parade and jack-o'-lantern carving contest. And I hear you can send a letter to the *real* Santa Claus, who just happens to live there.

It's a beautiful, historic place. I highly recommend visiting. Of course, it would help if I told you the name of the town, but what fun would that be? I know how you love a good mystery.

Dear Reader,

     I hope you have come to love these characters as much as I do. Nova Grant knocked around in my brain for years before she came to life on these pages. She is the perfect heroine—resourceful, brave, and able to suspend disbelief when faced with the unimaginable. Her sister, Alana, was created from memories I have of my own sister, who died at the age of 26.

     I've come to think of these characters as friends and family, often forgetting that they exist in a world of fantasy that I created. To me, they are real people, with distinct personalities and dreams of their own. Many of you have asked if I will ever revisit them now that the trilogy is complete. As Aunt Jean so aptly stated, "There are infinite possibilities…"

With gratitude,

Mary Rice

www.ingramcontent.com/pod-product-compliance
Lightning Source LLC
Chambersburg PA
CBHW032006060325
23041CB00004B/174